Hermann Beigel

The Human Hair

its structure, growth, diseases, and their treatment

Hermann Beigel

The Human Hair
its structure, growth, diseases, and their treatment

ISBN/EAN: 9783337368234

Printed in Europe, USA, Canada, Australia, Japan

Cover: Foto ©Andreas Hilbeck / pixelio.de

More available books at **www.hansebooks.com**

THE

HUMAN HAIR:

ITS STRUCTURE, GROWTH, DISEASES,

AND THEIR

TREATMENT.

Illustrated by Wood Engravings.

BY

HERMANN BEIGEL, M.D., M.R.C.P. Lond.

PHYSICIAN TO THE METROPOLITAN FREE HOSPITAL, TO THE FARRINGDON
AND TO THE ST. PANCRAS DISPENSARIES;
MEMBER OF THE PATHOLOGICAL, CLINICAL, OBSTETRICAL, AND
HUNTERIAN SOCIETIES, ETC. ETC.

HENRY RENSHAW,
356, STRAND, LONDON.
1869.

TO

DR. ERNEST HALLIER,

PROFESSOR OF BOTANY AT THE UNIVERSITY OF JENA,

IN ADMIRATION OF HIS GREAT TALENT

IN THE INVESTIGATION OF MISCROSCOPIC LIFE,

THIS LITTLE WORK IS

Respectfully Dedicated,

BY

THE AUTHOR.

PREFACE.

THE human hair being an ornament which it is almost
everybody's endeavour to preserve inviolate as long as
possible, it is explicable, why the fear of losing that
ornament has become a matter of speculation of charlatanism on the credulity of the public. The best
means of confounding the designs of such speculations,
is the statement of real facts, distributing thus the
light of knowledge.

The following pages are intended to be a popular
treatise, aiming at showing that the laws by which the
life of the hair is governed differ not from the laws to
which the body at large is subject, and that deviations
of normal development must be considered—as is the
case in other organs—as disease and treated as such.
Although this little book aims—as already mentioned—
at being a popular treatise, yet I hope that some of
the chapters may interest even those who have a knowledge of the subject, I allude to the chapter on the
chignon-fungus, and to that on cracking of the
hair, &c.

H. BEIGEL, M.D.

3, *Finsbury Square,*
    28th December, 1868.

TABLE OF CONTENTS.

THE HUMAN HAIR

IN

A STATE OF HEALTH AND DISEASE.

CHAPTER I.

HISTORICAL REMARKS.

FROM the remotest times, and by all nations, great importance has been attached to that appendix of the human body which is considered one of its finest ornaments; Julius Cæsar, the great Roman General, who, unfortunately, was bald-headed, considered therefore—according to the Roman historian Suetonius—of all the honours bestowed upon him by the Senate, that as the greatest, by virtue of which permission was granted to him to wear permanently his laurel in order to cover his deficiency of hair.

A head densely grown with hair has always been considered as a symbol of vigour and

B

strength. Thus Samson says to Delilah, "There hath not come a razor upon mine head. . . . . If I be shaven, then my strength will go from me, and I shall become weak, and be like any other man." And, indeed, " she made him sleep upon her knees ; and she called for a man, and she caused him to shave off the seven locks of his head ; and she began to afflict him, and his strength went from him."

Accordingly, "baldhead" was used as a strong term of reproach. Thus 2nd Kings, ii. 23, we read of Elisha, " And he went up from thence unto Bethel : and as he was going up by the way, there came forth little children out of the city, and mocked him, and said unto him, Go up, thou baldhead ; go up, thou baldhead." But one of the most degrading forms of expressing contempt amongst the ancient Jews was plucking off the hair. We find Nehemiah mentioning this as a punishment inflicted upon those who had contracted irregular marriages.

Shaving the head is often referred to by the Hebrew prophets, denoting metaphorically affliction, poverty, and disgrace.

We cannot therefore be astonished that war ensued from the offence given by the Prince of the Ammonites to the delegates of David in shaving off the one-half of their beards. The natural thinness or want of hair was the more dreaded because considered as the first stage of lepra, which excluded the afflicted individual from society, being compelled to live outside the precincts of the town.

The Arabs also consider a bald head as a disgrace, and therefore in the conclusion of their oath, when accused of some crime, they say : " If I have done it, then may the Lord turn my locks into a bald head." The Arabs value their hair so highly that they sacrifice it after each pilgrimage to Mecca in the valley of Mina, which ceremony forms the most solemn concluding act of the pilgrimage. In Greece, it was likewise customary to put the hair of a boy, when becoming a youth, upon the altar of a tutelar deity ; but this was done not only on the occasion just mentioned, but before any other serious or solemn undertaking—marriage, for instance—before a long journey, going to war, &c. On the graves of beloved ones the hair was laid down as a sacrifice, which was called the " mourning locks."

Thus the Levites—whose business it was to give to the priests all necessary assistance in the discharge of their duties, and to keep guard round the Tabernacle, and afterwards round the Temple—cut their hair when initiated into office, from which ceremony in the Roman Catholic Church the tonsure is preserved up to the present day.   It consists in shaving the crown of the head as a preparation for orders, and the higher the degree of priesthood the larger the tonsure that is required.   It is a curious fact that the Church was never favourable towards the wearing of long hair.   Pope Anicetus is said to have been the first who forbade the clergy to wear long hair, but the prohibition is of an older date in the churches of the East.   There is a canon still extant of 1096, importing that such as wore long hair should be excluded from coming into church while living, and not to be prayed for when dead, and in France under Hugh Capet the priests excommunicated all who let their hair grow.

St. Wulstan, Bishop of Worcester, declaimed

with great vehemence against luxury of all kinds, but chiefly against long hair as most criminal and most universal. "When any of those vain people," says William of Malmesbury, "bowed their heads before him, to receive his blessing, before he gave it he cut a lock of their hair with a little knife which he carried about with him for that purpose, and commanded them by way of penance of their sins, to cut all the rest of their hair in the same manner. If any of them refused to comply with his command, he denounced the most dreadful judgment upon them, reproached them for their effeminacy, and foretold that, as they imitated woman in the length of the hair, they would imitate them in their cowardice when their country was invaded, which was accomplished at the landing of the Normans."

Serlo, a Norman bishop, acquired great honour by a sermon which he preached before Henry I. in 1104, against long and curled hair, with which the King and all his courtiers were so much affected, that they consented to resign their flowing ringlets, of which they had been so vain. The preaching prelate gave them no time to change their minds, but immediately pulled a pair of shears out of his sleeve, and performed the operation with his own hand.*

Not only in the churches and confessionals has war been declared against long hair, but public discussions were held and volumes written about it. Thus, a professor of Utrecht in 1650, wrote expressly on the question, whether it be lawful for men to wear long hair? and accounted for the negative. Another divine, named Raves, who had written for the affirmative, replied to him. Whether the intention to exterminate long hair was dictated to old worn-out priests and professors by envy of an ornament of which they were deprived by various causes, is difficult to say; but it is remarkable that the early Egyptians, who were proverbial for their habits of cleanliness, likewise removed their hair as an incumbrance. All classes among that people, including the foreign slaves, were required to submit to this custom (Gen. xli. 14), and in place of Nature's covering they made use of wigs, the reticulated texture of the groundwork on which the hair was fastened

---

* "The Lond. Encyclopæd." 1829. Art. Hair.

allowing free circulation, while the hair effectually protected the head from the sun.*

According to Oriental notions the hair must be black and dense in order to be considered beautiful. Thus we find in Solomon's Song (v. 11)—" His head is as the most fine gold, his locks are bushy, and black as a raven."

Other poets compare the maiden's locks more frequently to the dark night in which her countenance shines brightly, like the silver moon ; and wicked Jezebel knew already well dressed hair to be a powerful help towards good looks, for when she heard of Jehu's coming to Jezreel, she painted her face, and attired her head, and looked out at a window (2nd Kings, ix. 30).

We know from the New Testament, that Mary did not consider her hair unworthy to wipe the feet of Jesus with at Bethany. The same was done to Him by the woman, the sinner, in the Pharisee's house : " She began to wash His feet with tears, and did wipe them with the hairs of her head."

---

* Wilkinson's " Anc. Egyptians," iii. 354.

It was a custom among the Greeks to hang
up the hair of their dead at the door to
prevent any one from defiling himself by
entering the house. This is in close connexion with another Greek custom of long
hair not only being a privilege of free men,
but its different lengths also denoting certain
positions in life. The Greeks, having the
most refined taste for everything that is
beautiful, considered the hair one of the finest
ornaments Nature has bestowed upon man,
and great attention was paid to its management. The first and principal sign of thraldom
was, therefore, forfeit of the privilege of
wearing long hair. This is, in a certain
degree, preserved up to the present time, in
so far as the hair of prisoners at their entering
the gaol is cut short. Even the citizens of
Sparta, where all ornamental attire was pro-
hibited by law, could not part with the one
which they considered the gift of nature ; and
by the way in which their hair was cut, clan,
rank, and age could be recognised. When
Charillus was asked why the Spartans wore
long hair ? he replied, " Because it is the
cheapest ornament." Curly hair was particu-

larly esteemed in Athens, and the hairdressers were at that time already busy in giving it artificially that shape, if it had not grown so naturally. Contrary to the Oriental taste the Greeks held fair hair as the finest; and the art of dyeing the hair, if not naturally light-coloured, was in those times already a very profitable business.

The Romans wore a long time the hair of the beard without shaving or cutting it, and the time is not exactly known when they began to do it. Thus Livius seems to tell us, that this custom was in use from the year 369, for, speaking of Manlius Capitolinus, who was taken prisoner, he relates that the greatest part of the people being troubled at his imprisonment, changed their clothes and let their beards and hair grow. If this were so, then we may infer that out of time of mourning they had their hair cut and their beards shaved. Nevertheless Varro speaks clearly, that the first barbers came out of Sicily to Rome in the year 454, and that a man called Ticinius Menas brought them. From that time the young men began to have their beards cut, and hair, till they became forty-nine years old, but it was not allowed to be done above that age, says Pliny. The day when young men were shaved for the first time was a day of rejoicing, and they were careful to put the hair of their beard into a silver or gold box, and to make an offering of it to some god, particularly to Jupiter Capitolinus, as Nero did, according to the testimony of Suetonius.*

The ancient Britons were proud of the length and beauty of their hair, and were at much pains in dressing it. A young warrior who was taken prisoner, and condemned to be beheaded, requested as the last and greatest favour, that no slave might be permitted to touch his hair, which was remarkably long and beautiful, and that it might not be stained with his blood.

Among the Frankish kings, says Gregory of Tours, it was long the peculiar privilege of the blood royal to have flowing locks, while for all other persons there were gradations in the lengths and peculiar cut of the hair, according to the rank, from the noble down to the close-cropped slave. When a prince was

---

* " Pantologia," vol. v.

excluded from the right of succession to the crown, his long locks were shorn to denote that he was reduced to the condition of a subject. From the time of Clovis, the French nobility wore the hair short, but as they grew less material they allowed it to grow longer.

Long hair was the prevailing fashion at the court of Francis I., when the king, proud of the wound of his head, appeared with short hair, and thereupon that style became general. Long hair again came into vogue in the reign of Louis XIII., and as curling was found inconvenient, wigs became fashionable. Then followed the reign of hair-powder, perriwigs, and perukes of enormous dimensions, which, together with many other things no less preposterous, were swept away in the tide of the great French Revolution.*

To refer to the customs of the different nations concerning the hair would result in a voluminous book, but the above remarks will suffice to show that the part played by the hair in ancient times has not been less important

---

* "Encyclop. Britannic.," vol. xi.

than it is at present.   This does not only
hold good in respect to natural but also to artificial hair, which was used not only by the
Egyptians, but also by the Greeks, the Cartha-
ginians, and especially by the Romans, amongst
whom the sale of human hair, particularly the
blond hair of Germany, was an ordinary species
of traffic. Dyeing the hair, too, was much practised by the Romans, and a kind of gold-dust
was used by the ladies who did not adopt
borrowed locks.   Josephus relates that King
Solomon's horseguards daily strewed their
heads with gold-dust which glittered in the
sun.*

In the present time the artificial hair trade
has assumed great proportions, and I think the
subject is interesting enough to justify the
following extract from an article in the *Daily
News :*—

"The statistics of the false hair trade
furnish curious evidence of the increased and
increasing artificiality of the age.   Male
wigs have gone out of fashion, and it is
the enormous quantities of false hair used by

---

* Josephus, "Antiq.," viii. 7.

ladies which have caused the vast rise in its price. This has gone up 400 per cent. within the last dozen years, while four times as much is used now as at that period. Sixteen times as much money is consequently spent upon this article of adornment in the present year as was devoted to it in 1856, a suggestive fact for the swains who are now admiring the silken tresses of their fair partners in the dance, or at the sea-side promenade. Those who only know false hair from the curious lumps of it in the hairdresser's windows, and from a general suspicion that they see it on the heads of some of their friends, cannot form a notion of the extent to which the trade in it is carried on. It has wholesale dealers with large warehouses, and skilled labourers constantly at work. It is manufactured to meet the wishes and the purses of all classes of society, from the sixpenny frizette sold to fill out the sparse locks of the servant-of-all-work, to the ten-guinea head of hair made up to aid the beauty of a duchess. The finest specimen of this elderly hair will sell for as much as two guineas an ounce; while the very best black or brown will sell from eighteen shillings to one guinea, and the best flaxen at about a guinea and a-half. The latter variety is, be the quality what it may, about fifty per cent. dearer than black or brown hair, while white or grey fetches more than the latter by 100 per cent. For it is unnecessary to say that much of the hair sold is far less expensive than that just quoted. Quality, colour, and length determine its price, which ranges from a few shillings an ounce upwards. After the hair has been combed and washed and dried, it is folded into oblong parcels, such as large skeins of silk or worsted that are kept in the shops. Fair Saxon hair is still greatly in demand, and, as the stock of it must be kept up, many of the other colours have to be stained to the favourite hue. But dyeing hair is far less easy when it has been cut from the head. The natural perspiration of the human subject acts with the chemical compounds used, and it is the boast of the fashionable hairdresser that he can change the hair to any colour by a few applications of his famous washes. The lady who had stained her hair to what she considered the fashionable colour had in many instances attained a tinge unlike any other thing on earth. When, therefore, she wanted a new chignon, or tresses to match her latest hue, it was impossible to procure them. No shade of flaxen but by the side of her own metallic yellow would seem dull and flat ; and the only way out of the difficulty was artificially to stain the hair a gold until it looked as unnatural as the hair growing. We should mention that a considerable trade exists in false beards, moustaches, and whiskers. During the American war a vast number of these were sent out to the United States, and a steady demand continued until the peace. Our informant did not profess to account either for the sudden want of whiskers and beards, or for its equally sudden cessation. But the fact is curious, that the demand lasted as long as the war, and gradually dropped off at its close. The moustache and whisker, like the best wig fronts and scalps, are based upon a fine network of white hair, through which the skin of the wearer shows, and a ' parting' is secured which fairly rivals Nature. Our investigations have been made among some of the largest wholesale dealers in human hair, as well as at some of the most fashionable retail shops.

Both abound in the metropolis. The penalty
of such inquiries is, that they inevitably leave
a hideous doubt upon the mind of the reality
of the curls, or chignons, or tresses. When
art imitates Nature so wonderfully, and where
—as figures and professional witnesses prove
to us—a large proportion of the female popu-
lation avail themselves of art, it becomes ex-
ceedingly difficult to draw the line between
the two. After seeing and handling hair
taken from many thousands of heads, and
being taught its use, the belief is pardonable,
if morbid, that false locks are almost as common as real, and that whenever they are especially beautiful they should awaken most
distrust."

CHAPTER II.

THE mere aspect of the hair by the unaided eye gives no information whatever in respect to its structure; it seems to consist of homogeneous matter variously coloured in different hairs, having a thread-like shape, the one end being bulbiform, like a little knob, the other end, the *tip* of a hair, if not cut previously, being the finest part of the whole hair, thus presenting the smallest circumference. A pin, therefore, would be the most appropriate pattern of a hair's shape, the pin's head representing the *bulb*, the point of the pin representing the *tip* of the hair, and the part of the pin between the point and the head representing the hair's *shaft*. That would be nearly all the information we could gain by ocular inspection, and all conditions concerning minute structure, growth, disease, &c., would not become known to us—nay, we

c

should even remain ignorant on all matters respecting the colour of the hair, if we were not able to penetrate into the different layers and tissues, in order not only to study their structure, but also to observe the action upon them of different chemical agencies.

The microscope is that most valuable instrument which enables us to trace the works of Nature to their first origin, and to study Nature's most remarkable and at the same time invariable and unchangeable laws. It is not my purpose to dwell here on the pleasure and satisfaction which microscopic researches give, nor is it my task to show how necessary it is for every well-educated man to make himself acquainted at least with the rudimentary phenomena of Nature which surround him daily, hourly, nay, every second; by which he lives, breathes, moves, sees, hears, &c., phenomena which make the knowledge of microscopic work indispensable. But for the purpose I have in view it will suffice just to give the general rules for the use of the microscope, in order to enable the reader to examine hair and preserve it on slides (fig. 2), for it would be a very erroneous conception to think that the mere possession of a microscope renders the possessor fit for microscopic examination. Oh no; microscopy is an art, requiring instruction, dexterity, experience, and, like any other art, must be taught and acquired by practical work.

Those, however, who wish to get a thorough knowledge of microscopy must be referred to Dr. Lionel Beale's excellent work, " How to Work with the Microscope," or to the works of Carpenter, Quekett, Harley, and others. But for those who are anxious to gain such information as will enable them not only to follow the researches on which I shall have to treat, but also to acquire the necessary dexterity in order to set to work themselves, the following remarks may form an introduction to their studies.

For examination of the hair and similar structures no expensive instrument is required. A microscope which enlarges about two or three hundred times will suit all purposes.

The principal part of the microscope is the tube A B (fig. 1), both extremities containing lenses, those at A forming the eye-piece, and those at B the object glasses; C is the stage on which the slides are put for examination, and on which light is thrown by the

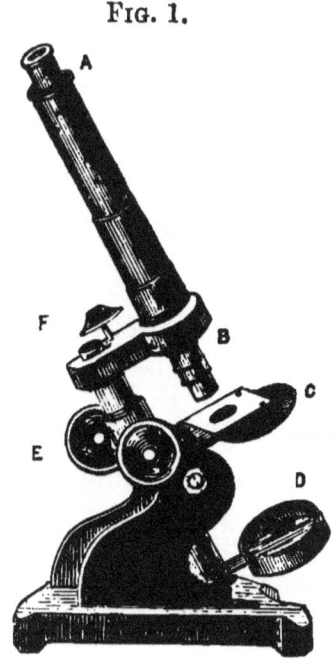

FIG. 1.

mirror D ; the coarse adjustment is effected by the screws at C, and the finer adjustment by that at F.

Large microscopes have generally three eye-pieces, marked A, B, C, and a number of object-glasses, from two inches to a fiftieth of an inch. These numbers have reference to the *focal distance*, which term means the distance of the object-glasses B from the object to be examined. Thus a two-inch objective means a combination of lenses which have the magnifying power of a single lens, the focal point of which is two inches from the object.

The magnifying power of a microscope may be seen in the following table :—

Eye-pieces.	Object-glasses.								
	2 in.	1 iu.	½ in.	¼ in.	⅛ in.	$\frac{1}{12}$ in.	$\frac{1}{16}$ in.	$\frac{1}{23}$ in.	$\frac{1}{50}$ in.
A	20	60	100	220	420	600	800	1250	2500
B	30	80	130	350	670	870	1184	1850	3700
C	40	100	180	500	900	1400	1500	2500	5000

The combination of eye-piece A with the 2 in. objective constitutes therefore a magnifying power of 20. Eye-piece B with the same objective magnifies 30 times ; eye-piece C with the same objective 40 times, and so forth. These measurements are linear—that means, the object which is magnified 200 times is as large as if 200 such objects were laid down in one line. The microscope, however, does not magnify in one direction only, but in all directions alike ; the enlargement is therefore *superficial,* which is the square of the linear, consequently if the quarter-inch magnifies an object about 200 diameters, or 200 linears, its superficial measurement will be obviously the square of the 200 linears—namely, 40,000.

There are a few other instruments required for examination of the hair, namely :—

1. One or two sharp razors for making sections.
2. A common scalpel.
3. A fine sharp pair of scissors.
4. Needles, mounted on handles, as commonly used for microscopic work.
5. A pair of forceps.

The following chemicals are likewise necessary :—

1. Absolute alcohol.
2. Glycerine.
3. Turpentine.
4. Ether.
5. Sulphuric acid.
6. Nitric acid.
7. Hydrochloric acid.
8. A solution of potash.
9. A solution of soda.

FIG. 2.

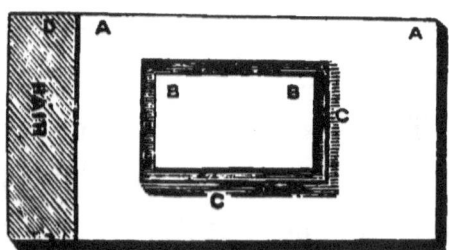

A few watch-glasses, two or three glass tubes, pieces of cork, glass slides (A A, fig. 2), glass covers (B B, fig. 2), and a few painting brushes, make the apparatus complete.

In order to examine a hair or a piece of hair, it is put on the slide and covered, while a few drops of alcohol are allowed to flow between the cover and the slide, whereby the air, filling the hair and preventing our seelng the structure, will escape, and allow the proper examination of the object.

CHAPTER III.

WHEN a farmer wishes to gain a knowledge of the structure and physiology of the plants he takes so much pains to cultivate, he is obliged to study the composition of the soil, upon which the growth and development of the plants depend, and to learn its chemical and physical properties.

That is exactly the course we have to pursue in our researches. Being about to investigate the nature and development of the human hair, we are obliged to glance at the principal features of the soil which nourishes the hair, in which the hair has its root, and which, when it becomes diseased, very often imparts this condition to the hair, which then loses its glossy appearance, splits, becomes brittle, breaks off or falls out, together with its root, and causes a bald state of its former soil. The human skin, into which the roots of the hair are implanted is, with the exception of a few spots, all over covered with hair. These exceptional spots, where no hair grows, are the eyelids, the rosy parts of the lips, the palm of the hand, the sole of the foot, the dorsal side of the last joints of the fingers and toes, and one or two other smaller spots.

The skin forms a perfectly closed sac around the body, and having to discharge several duties, is of such great importance as to bring an individual's life into jeopardy if more than half becomes incapable of discharging these duties.

The following woodcut (fig. 3) shows the rough outlines of the microscopical appearances of a vertical section of the skin.

The structure of the human skin, with its tubes and glands and other organs, may well be compared with the ground on which large cities are built, as we see it sometimes in the streets of London when dug up for repairing the road or the water-pipes, and similar purposes.

When the upper layer of a street has been removed, we see a vast number of pipes, strings, canals, &c., running across or along each other, and serving several purposes. Here is a gutta

FIG. 3.*

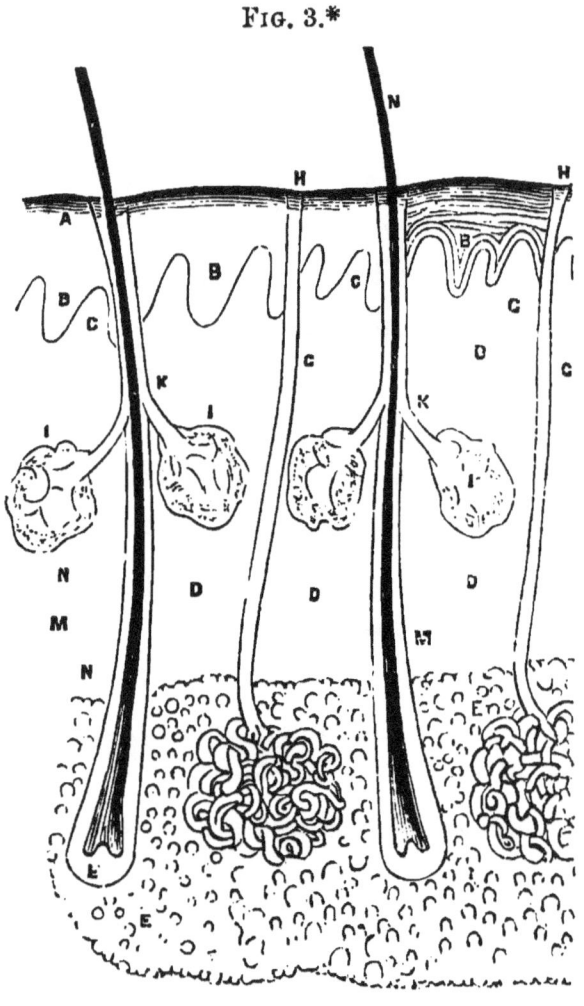

* Fig. 3 represents the outlines of a vertical section through the human skin, A A being the epidermis adapting itself to the elevations (C C) and depressions (B B) of the sensitive layer; C C, papillæ of the corium, D D; E E, fat deposited in the lower meshes of the corium; F F, globular balls of perspiratory apparatus; G G, tubes of the same apparatus; H H, openings of these tubes on the skin, called *pores;* I I, oil glands of the skin; K K, their openings into the sheath of the hair; L L, papillæ of the root of the hair; M M, sheath of the hair; N N, bulb and shaft of the hair.

percha covered wire for the telegraph, discharging electric duties; there is a pipe conveying gas or water to the houses, while the large canal carries away the refuse from the dwellings to a distant part of the Thames. Let these tubes become unfit for their respective work, and it will scarcely be possible to live in that vast city, and the health and lives of the inhabitants would become endangered. But in the proper, regular condition all these arrangements will do their work without interfering with each other, though they are imbedded in the same soil, now running parallel, now crossing and recrossing their course. This is exactly the case with the human skin constituting the surface of the body. It can distinctly be shown to be composed of three principal layers—namely, the *epidermis, the sensitive layer, and the corium.* The upper layer of the London ground, which must be removed before we can see the tubes and pipes, and the relation they bear to each other, would be represented in the skin by the *epidermis.* This is a semi-transparent membrane formed wholly of cells, and containing neither vessels nor nerves; it applies itself to all the elevations and depressions by which the sensitive layer of the corium is marked. If we therefore put a blister to the skin, whereby the epidermis, by means of a certain fluid, becomes separated from the corium, the separated part may easily and painlessly be cut and removed by a pair of scissors, representing an exact cast of the surface of the sensitive layer of the corium ; the convexities and concavities, of course, being in the same manner reversed in the epidermis as if you take a wax cast from a piece of money.

The sensitive layer—called the Malpighian stratum—lies between the epidermis and the corium ; it is but thin and uneven, composed of numerous vessels, upon which the colour of the skin depends. Low temperature causes them to contract, whereby the skin assumes a pale or dusky appearance, while they expand in high temperature, and, the supply of blood hereby becoming increased, give to the skin a red hue. The unevenness of that layer, says Erasmus Wilson, has reference to an important law in animal organization—namely, that of multiplying surface for the increase of friction ; and the means of effecting this object is by the extension of its substance into little, elongated, conical prominences, technically termed papillæ. These papillæ in certain parts, as in the palms of the hands, are raised in the form of small ridges, which can be seen by the naked eye.

The *corium* is composed of a firm tissue ; its lower meshes contain fat globules, which for the economy of our body are of the highest importance.

The three layers just mentioned contain besides a vast number of nerves, which render the skin the organ of touch, and vessels giving to the skin its hue, certain tubular or glandular apparatus, the former for perspiratory purposes, the latter in order to keep the surface of the skin bedewed with an oily fluid.

These tubes traverse the three layers of the skin more or less deeply, and open on the surface of the epidermis as very minute apertures, which we know under the name of *pores.* In healthy life, the perspiratory apparatus, consisting of small tubes, and terminating in little globular balls, removes the excess of water and of certain salts dissolved in the blood, and regulates the temperature of the latter. This process, which is constantly

going on, has been called *insensible perspiration.*
In disease, however, or when the body undergoes great muscular exercise, that fluid forms
drops on the skin, and is known to us as *sweat.*

But the question might be raised whether
a number of small tubes, which can be seen
only by means of a microscope, are really of any
importance in the economy of our body? In
order to arrive at something like an estimate
of the value of the perspiratory system in relation to the rest of the organism, Erasmus
Wilson counted the perspiratory pores on the
palm of the hand, and found 3528 of them in
a square inch. "Now," he continues, "each
of these pores being the aperture of a little
tube about a quarter of an inch long, it follows
that in a square inch of skin on the palm of
the hand there exists a length of tube equal
to 882 inches, or 73½ feet. Surely such an
amount of drainage as seventy-three feet in
every square inch of skin, assuming this to be
the average of the whole body, is something
wonderful, and the thought naturally intrudes
itself—What if this drainage were obstructed?
Could we need a stronger argument for en-
forcing the necessity of attention to the skin.

" On the pulps of the fingers, where the ridges of the sensitive layer of the true skin are somewhat finer than in the palm of the hand, the number of pores on a square inch a little exceeded that of the palm, and on the heel, where the ridges are coarser, the number of pores on a square inch was 2268, and the length of tube 567 inches, or forty-seven feet. To obtain an estimate of the length of tube of the perspiratory system of the whole surface of the body, I think that 2800 might be taken as a fair average of the number of pores in the square inch, and 700, consequently, of the number of inches in length. *Now the number of square inches of surface in a man of ordinary height and bulk, is 2500; the number of pores, therefore, seven millions, and the number of inches of perspiratory tube one million seven hundred and fifty thousand— that is, one hundred and forty-five thousand eight hundred and thirty-three feet, or forty-eight thousand six hundred yards, or nearly twenty-eight miles.*"

CHAPTER IV.

MICROSCOPICAL STRUCTURE OF THE HAIR.

EVERY day's observation teaches us that moistening of the skin with water causes the latter to form in drops, as if thrown on an oily surface. The skin is, in fact, nothing else but such a fat surface, and it has already been mentioned that it contains a separate apparatus, which has to discharge the duty of keeping the surface of the skin bedewed with an oily fluid. The general structure of this apparatus resembles that of the perspiratory system, consisting of fine tubes and small glands, the latter imbedded in the corium, the former traversing the sensitive layer, and terminating as minute openings in the epidermis or scarf.

The fourth formation implanted in the skin, is the hair. It may be regarded as a modification of the epidermis, to which it is analogous in mode of formation, but than which it is somewhat more highly organized and complex.

The root of each hair is implanted into the subcutaneous fat-layer of the skin, and as far as running through the skin, is involved in a sheath (fig. 3, м, м) called the *hair sac*, which may be considered simply as an involu·tion of the skin with the epidermis and the layers of the corium.

Pulling out a hair from the skin, some layers of the sac, firmly adhering to it, are likewise torn out while other layers, closely attached to the skin, remain behind.

The root is of a softer consistence than the rest of the hair, and has sometimes a reddish, sometimes a gray or black colour. Its shape, as already stated, is bulbous, or rather club-like, because of its projecting into the hair-shaft.

The following woodcut (fig. 4), represents the root of the hair, · together with the hair-sacs (*f*), the root sheath (*d, c*), and the *papilla of the hair* (*h*).

These parts are of the utmost importance, inasmuch as from them the hair's growth takes place. We must therefore make ourselves thoroughly acquainted with their structure, in order to be enabled to gain an insight into the physiology, and more particularly into the

D

diseases to which the hair is subject, and on which we shall have to treat hereafter.

FIG. 4.

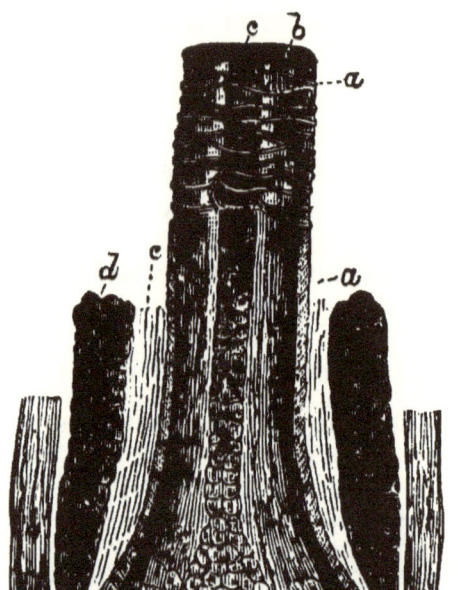

In each hair-sac there can be distinguished an external fibrous part (*f*), the proper hair-sac, and a non-vascular cellular investment lining this—the epidermis of the hair-sac—and the *root-sheath* (*d* and *c*), so termed because of its immediately surrounding the hair.

The proper hair-sac (*f*) consists of two fibrous layers, an external and an internal and of a structureless membrane, which contains in its lower part the *papilla of the hair* (*h*). Of these three layers the *external fibrous membrane* is the thickest; it determines on the form of the hair-sac, and is very closely attached to the corium.

The *internal fibrous membrane* is much more delicate than the external. It extends from the bottom of the hair-sac to the sebaceous glands. The third layer is a transparent membrane, which, when the hair is torn out, invariably remains behind in the hair-sac and extends from its base, though, as it would seem, without covering the papilla, as far as the inner root-sheath, and perhaps higher up.

Just from the ground of the sac the *papilla of the hair* projects, less properly termed the *hair germ*, corresponding with a papilla of the cutis. It consists of two parts, the one being a globular projection, or the proper papilla of the hair, the other consisting of a layer of cells covering the papilla, and gradually passing over into the middle membrane of the sac.

The *hair-sheath* (*d* and *c*) consists of two distinct layers, the external and internal, and thus forms a kind of lining membrane to the sac (*f*).

The external layer, or the external root-sheath (*d*), consists of very small round or oval-shaped cells, which, in several layers, lie upon another, and higher up pass over it into Malpighi's net-work, while at the bottom of the hair-sac they pass continuously and without any sharp line of demarcation, into the round cells of the hair-bulb which covers the papilla.

The *inner transparent root-sheath* (*c*) is half as thin as the outer; it extends almost from the hair-sac over more than two-thirds of it, and then suddenly ceases. It is externally closely connected with the outer root-sheath (*d*), internally with the cuticle of the hair (*a*).

In the root, the vital point of a hair, we have therefore to distinguish—

1. *The bulb of the hair substance.*

2. *Its immediate envelopment, the cuticle of the hair* (*a*).

3. *The inner root-sheath* (*c*).

4. *The external root-sheath* (*d*).

5. *The hair-sac,* consisting of three layers (*f*)·

6. *The papilla of the hair* (*h*).

These are the principal parts of the root of the hair, but there are several other structures, the investigation of which does not belong to our province, and will be undertaken by such readers only as intend to make themselves more intimately acquainted with the microscope than is the object of this book.

It remains only in conclusion to say a few words concerning the method of preparing the hair for examination under the microscope, and seeing the parts just described.

For that purpose it is necessary to use a piece of fresh calf's skin, hardened in a solution of chromic acid (about three grains of the acid to an ounce of water). In this solution the skin remains for about two or three days, after which it is hard enough for making sections of it by means of a sharp razor.

To make sections as fine as requisite for microscopical examination, some practice is required, which, however, can easily be acquired. Whoever does not like to wait until he is capable of making proper sections, may make use of the double-knife, an instrument much used in microscopy. It is in fact nothing but a knife with two blades, which, by means of a screw, may easily be brought at a very small distance from each other. If a cut is made by that knife into animal tissue, the piece remaining between the two blades is just a fit section for microscopic examination. If the skin of a calf is used for a section, the shape of the hair-bulb will be somewhat different from that in man, but the relation of the tissues is the same.

The shape of the hair-bulb differs not only in various animals, but even in the same animal, and in men when taken from different parts of the body. To examine the hair-sheath, it suffices to tear out a strong, thick hair from the beard, and the hair-sheath adhering to the bulb will likewise come off. If put in a very weak solution of caustic soda, or potash—five grains to the ounce of distilled water—and examined under the microscope, the external and internal sheath become very distinct.

We now come to the parts constituting the hair-shaft. If a hair be taken from the head and put under the microscope, nothing would be seen but a dark stroke without any structure. But if a few drops of alcohol be allowed to pass between the object-glass and the cover, or if we apply certain acids or alkalies, then a clear image is presented to our view, which shows the hair's minute composition, with all its particulars.

The reason why we have seen nothing of the structure of the hair before using the alcohol is because the hair contains, as will be seen, a great amount of air, which interferes with the transparency, and when driven out and replaced by the alcohol, admits of a clear view.

The hair thus prepared shows at the first glance three different cellular structures, as seen in fig. 5.

The exterior layer consists of cells covering the hair in a similar manner as do tiles the roof of a house, but not so regular. This layer is termed the *cuticle of the hair* (fig. 5, *b*, and fig. 4, *a*).

Next is seen the formation, presenting a longitudinal, striated appearance (*a*, and fig. 4, *b*). This being composed of differently-shaped cells, and being the real substance of the hair, is called the *cortical or fibrous substance of the hair.*

FIG. 5.

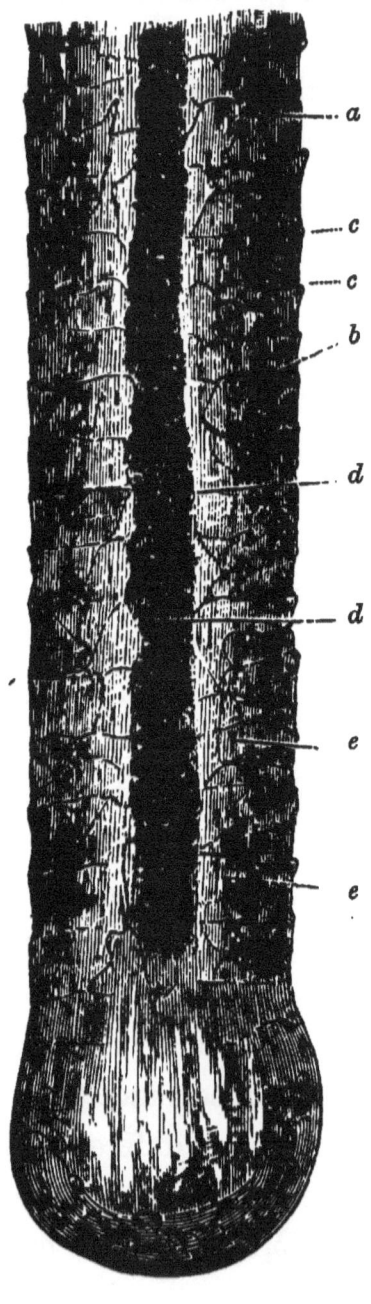

The third formation appears as a regular streak or cord, which extends in the central axis of the hair from the bulb to nearly the point of the hair (*d*, and fig. 4, *c*). This is called the *medullary substance of the hair.*

Besides, we see all over the hair some irregularly-distributed dark spots, which, as we shall learn, contain air, and have an important bearing on the question of the colour of the hair (*e e*).

1. *The cuticle* being, as already mentioned, the outer layer of the hair, is a very thin, transparent pellicle of flattened cells or scales of an oval form, completely investing the hair, and very closely united with the cortical substance. It becomes visible in all its details when treated by a solution of caustic soda, caustic potash, or by sulphuric acid.

The cells are so disposed that each inferior circle overlies the superior (*c c*), whereby the contours of the hair exhibit a serrated appearance. The scales of a fish or of a serpent would give a good idea of the arrangement, with the difference only that in these animals the plates are arranged with perfect regularity, which is not the case with the scales of the hair.

The interspaces of these irregular circular lines are a 2000th or 6000th part of a line from one another. Kölliker, a renowned German microscopist, is of opinion that the cuticle of the hair passes into the outer cells of the bulb. To this opinion Busk and Huxley object, and recommend the application of caustic ammonia as particularly fitted to demonstrate the structure of this part. In the first place, these excellent microscopists say, it raises up the outer layer of the cuticle from the inner, and shows that the former, at any rate, is not continuous with any cells; and secondly, it dissolves and forces out the substance of the lower soft portion of the bulb, so that the lower part of the cuticle may be obtained as a transparent, colourless, and independent sheath even from the very darkest hair. Lastly, under favourable circumstances, this reagent raises up a definite basement-membrane from the outer surface of the lowest part of the bulb, in immediate contact with the rounded " nuclei" of this part, and this basement-membrane may be traced upward into direct continuity with the homogeneous portion of the cuticle above described.

The scaly, tile-like construction of the cuticle explains the well-known phenomenon of the hair feeling rough when drawn between the fingers in one direction, and smooth on the opposite, or the spiral movement of a hair when drawn longitudinally between one finger, say the index, and the nail of the thumb. There is likewise due to this structure of the cuticle the firmness with which, on the one hand, hair, when cut, adheres to the neck and body, and on the other, with which dust and dirt, or particles of scurf, adhere to the hair.

A more important consequence, says Erasmus Wilson, of the projection of the edges of the scales which form its exterior surface, is the fact that the process of *felting* depends upon this peculiarity. Without it, hair would be unfitted, from the smoothness of its surface and shortness of its staple, for combining with the strength requisite for the production of felt. But in this fitness for felting there is great variety in hair, and an equal difference in the degree of prominence of its raised edges. In human hair they are very slightly marked; but nevertheless felting is not uncommon when the hair is neglected, and there are some diseases of the hair which turn wholly on this property of felting. When particles of dust collect on the edges of the scales and form projections, or the edges themselves become loosened and raised, they give the idea of branches from the shaft of the hair, an appearance which misled Leeuwenhoek into the belief that hairs, like feathers, were naturally furnished with branches.

2. *The cortical or fibrous substance.*—If a hair has been treated with caustic soda, or sulphuric acid, a pressure on the cover will suffice to separate the different layers of the cortical substance upon which the shape of the hair principally depends. In white hair, which, on account of its transparency, is particularly apt for microscopical examination, the cortical substance will be seen longitudinally striated, more so near the bulb, less towards the point. If a hair, after having been acted upon by sulphuric acid, is teased out by means of needles, it is not at all difficult to separate lace-like, lance-shaped cells, showing a lighter or darker yellow or brownish hue. These cells are not yet the ultimate elements of the cortical substance, but when the action of the

acid continues, may be subdivided into spindle-shaped spicula, these being the proper cells of the substance. In darker hair these cells contain pigment-molecules, which are sometimes accumulated to more or less extensive groups. From these groups other dark spots, likewise abundantly seen in these cells, must be distinguished as small holes filled with air. That they have nothing to do with the pigment-molecules, becomes evident by the fact of their principally being present in white hair, which is void of all pigment, and of the holes becoming filled with turpentine after the escape of the air, if the hair has been put for a certain time into that fluid.

The escape of air takes place in a more rapid manner, and offers a very amusing spectacle, if, instead of putting the hair into turpentine, a drop of muriatic acid is allowed to flow between the cover and the object-glass. As soon as that is done, large air-bubbles may be seen to escape from the medullary canal and the air spaces of the cortical substance, and to surround the hair. According to the description given of the structure of the cortical substance, it will be easily explicable why the flow of air bubbles is much more active near the bulb than at more distant parts of the hair. The dark spots then disappear, the dark cells, forming the medullary canal, become transparent, but assume their former condition when the action of the acid ceases, and the hair is washed in water and dried in the air.

No one who undertakes to study the structure of the hair ought to neglect this experiment, which gives him an idea of the great amount of air contained in and between the tissues of the hair. This arrangement being—as already stated—of great importance in respect to the question of the colour of the hair, it is necessary to be well acquainted with it before entering on that question.

Having considered the structure of the cuticle of the hair, and of the cortical substance as revealed by the microscope, we have now to examine the third kind of tissue, namely—

3. *The medullary substance of the hair* (fig. 5, *d d*).—It forms, as already stated, a streak or cord through nearly the whole axis of the hair, appearing dark when viewed by the

microscope ; being absent in the hair of young children, and in very fine thin hair generally, but always being present in strong hair, particularly when grey or white.

Writers differ very much in respect to the nature and structure of the medullary cord. Formerly it was considered to be composed of tubes, which, taking rise in the bulb of the hair, and running through its axis, are filled with an oily fluid to keep the hair soft and smooth.

At present we know well that it is air which has formerly been considered colouring matter by some, and a fluid by others.

As I have remarked on a former occasion, we may drive out the air contained in the central tube—as the medullary cord has likewise been called—and see it re-enter again under the microscope. This can be done in different ways. Turpentine penetrates all parts of the hair which are filled by air, but its action is slow and requires some time. If we put therefore a hair into turpentine, and allow it to remain therein about twenty-four hours, and view it under the microscope, we find the central tube, which was dark until acted upon by turpentine, light—perfectly transparent. But if we expose the hair again to a high temperature, the turpentine evaporates, and becomes replenished by air, consequently the central tube assumes its dark appearance again.

The same phenomenon may at once be observed when we boil a hair in nitric acid, or in a mixture of equal parts of nitric acid and hydrochloric acid. In this instance, the air-vesicles, which are of such an extremely small size as to make the impression of a uniform dark streak, become confluent, forming large air-bubbles, and filling more or less regularly the central tube. These air-bubbles, I think, have been mistaken by some authors for medullary cells, which I have failed to discover, though I have searched for them with care. What I have seen is this. When the central tube has been deprived of the air contained therein, we see a transparent streak running through the centre of the hair, consisting apparently of extremely minute meshes. These meshes must either be in communication with each other, or have such a construction of their walls as to allow the air to pass from one mesh or cell to the other. For when making the experiment just alluded to— viz., of driving out the air by turpentine and allowing it to enter again—one sees the air moving along the central tube with great rapidity, finding resistance nowhere.

The part of the medulla immediately above the bulb is generally of a pale appearance, containing no air. Such pale spots may likewise be found in the course of the streak, thus interrupting its continuity.

Another phenomenon easily observable is the division of the medullary cord into two parts, forming two streaks, which either have a separate course all along from the root through the shaft, or which run a certain distance as separate cords, and then unite again in one.

The medullary substance generally occupies a fourth or fifth part of the hair's breadth; its breadth is the greatest in short thick hair, least in the down and hair of the head. In a transverse section it presents a round or flattened figure, and the cells which comprise it are disposed in one or more longitudinal series.

In animals the central tube very often consists of large air-cells, ranging one after the other, either in close juxtaposition, or with dark spaces between the one cell and the other; one such cell, in some instances, being so large as to occupy the whole breadth of the medulla. Although the central part of the hair of man, says Wilson, is a loose pith, in which the original spherical form of the cells is more or less completely lost, yet in many animals this form is retained with the most exact precision, and such hairs appear to contain on their axis a very beautiful string of beads, rendered strikingly obvious, in dried hairs, by the emptiness of the cells. Such is the appearance of the very fine hairs of the hare or mouse. In thick hairs from the same animals, there are two or three or more rows of cells, and the largest hairs, from the number of these rows, bear a resemblance in structure to an ear of maize. This is the chief modification which the pith of the hair undergoes in the animal kingdom, being more or less completely cellulated, and holding a greater or lesser proportion to the entire bulk of the hair; sometimes, indeed, from one of the deer-tribe, the whole texture of the hair is cellular, the other two portions being condensed into a thin envelope. In the feather of a bird, which is a modification of the hair, the white pith, with its dense external covering, is very evident in the shaft, while the quill is an illustration of the outer parts alone, the transparent puckered membrane, which is drawn out of the quill when first cut, being a single row of dried-up cells. In the growing feather, the contents of the quill would be found distinctly cellulated.

The arrangement of a central tube in the axis of the hair adds a great deal to the elasticity of the hair, while it diminishes its weight; and yet the hair is of considerable strength, which depends upon the properties of the cortical or fibrous substance. A single hair from a boy eight years of age, says Robinson, in his " Essays on Natural Economy," supported a weight of 7812 grains; and from a man aged twenty-two, 14,285 grains; and a hair from a man of fifty-seven, 22,222 grains. Muschenbroeck found that a human hair, fifty-seven times thicker than a silkworm's thread, would support a weight of 2069 grains; and a horse's hair, seven times thicker, 7970 grains.   A part of this extraordinary strength is undoubtedly due to the high degree of elasticity which it possesses.

Withof considers two ounces to be the greatest weight the human hair can bear. A hair taken from the head, and measuring five inches, broke when the weight was nearly three ounces.

A hair 8 in. long broke by the weight of $2\frac{1}{2}$ ounces.

„	11 in.	„	„	$2\frac{3}{8}$	„
„	12 in.	„	„	$2\frac{1}{7}$	„
„	14 in.	„	„	$2\frac{1}{8}$	„

It is therefore evident that a hair bears easily two ounces weight. According to Haller, from the eighth to the twenty-second year of age, the strength of the hair increases from 10,309 to 12,967 parts, and up to the fifty-seventh year to 25,000 parts. E. H. Weber, the celebrated physiologist, found the human hair as elastic as india-rubber, but after elongation it remains elongated to a certain extent. He found the hair of a lady thirty-five years of age, capable of expanding about one-third of its natural length. Such being the strength of the human hair, we find in history very often that women sacrificed their finest ornament, the hair, in order to make ropes and bows *pro patria.* It was for such a sacrifice, made by the women of Rome when that city was besieged by the Gauls, that the Roman senate ordered the erection of the temple *Veneris calvæ* in honour of the patriotic behaviour of the women of Rome.

CHAPTER V.

DEVELOPMENT OF THE HAIR.

In the human embryo, the first rudiments of
the hairs become visible at the end of the
third or the beginning of the fourth month.
They are constantly first to be seen upon the
forehead and eyebrows, and consist of papilli-
form masses of cells, which may be recognised
even by the naked eye, as minute whitish
spots. The roundish, partly elongated cells
of which they consist, measure about a
four-thousandth part of a line, and resemble
closely the cells of the cutis, with which
they are, indeed, in constant connexion.

Fig. 6.

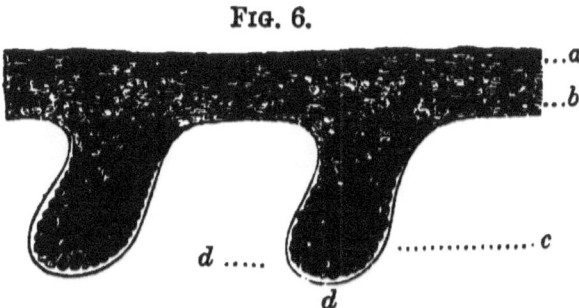

Fig. 6 represents such rudiments of hairs

from the brow of a human embryo sixteen weeks old, drawn after Kölliker, by an enlargement of 350 diameters; *a* representing the horny layers of the epidermis, *b* its mucous layer, *c* the structureless membrane surrounding the rudiment of the hair, and by its continuation between the mucous layer of the corium, forming the constant connexion just mentioned ; *d*, roundish, partly-elongated cells, which especially compose the rudiments of the hair.

At about the fifteenth week the structureless membrane may be seen formed around these cell-masses, which membrane, according to Kölliker, afterwards remains the inner structureless membrane of the hair-sac. Somewhat later, new cells develop upon the outer surface of the membrane, which in the course of development assume the shape of those microscopical elements which we already know as the two outer layers of the hair-sac.

Within the structureless membrane the cells become elongated, the peripheral ones more in a vertical, the central in a horizontal direction, as seen in the figure above (*d d*). In the central cells the elongation increases constantly, and at the end of the eighteenth month they form a light cone, which may easily be distinguished from the layer of peripheral cells. The basis of the cone rests on the floor of the structureless little sac, while its point projects towards the upper surface.

This light cone, after the hair-rudiments have attained a length of the twenty-five hundredth part of a line, becomes divided into two structures—a central portion somewhat darker, and an external one, perfectly transparent and glassy, the former turning horny, thus becoming transformed into the real hair, while the latter forms the inner layer of the sheath of the root. Between these layers and the structureless envelopment of the original cell-masses are the peripheral cells, mentioned above as the outer layer of the sheath of the root. At the same time, at the basis of the cone the papilla of the hair becomes visible as a small heap of light cells.

Thus the hairs of the embryo lie enveloped in the structureless little sac, the tips covered by the epidermis, through which (fig. 7) they eventually make their passage.

Fig. 7 illustrates the facts just treated of; it represents a rudimental hair from the eye-

FIG. 7.

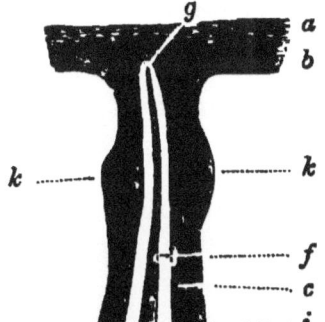

brows with a just developed, but not yet erupted, hair 0·28 of a line in length; the inner root-sheath projecting beyond the hair somewhat at the upper part, and laterally at the neck of the sac. The first rudiments of the sebaceous glands appear in the form of two papillary outgrowths from the outer root-sheath (*k k*). *a* is the horny layer of the epidermis; *b*, mucous layer; *c*, outer root-sheath of the subjacent sac; *i*, structureless membrane upon its outer side; *h*, papilla of the hair ; *f,* hair-shaft ; *g,* hair-point ; *k k,* rudiments of the sebaceous glands.*

These downy hairs are technically termed Lanugo, the eruption of which is completed between the twenty-third and twenty-fifth week. After the eruption they grow slowly to a length of one-fourth to one-third of a line, and to a greater length upon the head than elsewhere.

After birth a total shedding of the hair takes place, in consequence of the development of new hairs within the hair sacs of the lanugo, which gradually force out the old ones. This shedding, according to Kölliker, whose investigations have thrown light on all these points, commences by an out-growth of the soft round cells of the bulb and of the neighbouring outer root-sheath, from the bottom of the sacs of the lanugo, into long processes composed of cells, by which the hair is raised from its papilla, whilst at the same time it becomes converted into horn, even in its lowermost portion. The young hair thrusts upwards the bulb of the old hair, until at last

---

* From Kölliker.

it passes completely out, and makes its appearance by the same opening as the old one, which is more and more pushed up. If we therefore examine the skin of children of one or two years of age, we find that every hair-sac contains two hairs, of which the embryonal one lies uppermost, containing no root-sheath, whilst the newly-formed hair is found to lie beneath the former.

When the development of the hair has gone thus far, the old hair, which for a long time has ceased to grow, and to be connected with the bottom of the sac, being thus extruded, falls out, while the young hair becomes larger and stronger, filling the gap left by the old one. Herewith the whole process is completed.

The hair thus developed is not—and this is very important to know—a dead substance. It is no doubt nourished and maintained by certain fluids, furnished from the vessels of the papilla, which, when wanting, cause the hair to lose its glossy appearance, becoming cleft and brittle. Here we find an answer to the question, raised over and over again— namely, whether a hair may become diseased.

From the facts hitherto treated of, we shall at once be able to answer a second question—namely, whether hair, when lost by some disease or otherwise, can grow again ? The whole growth of the hair having, as we have just seen, its origin on the papilla of the hair within the sac, the question will be whether the loss of hair has been a consequence of the destruction of the sac and papilla, or of other causes, whereby the hair-sacs, together with their papillæ, have been preserved. If the former be the case, *no power on earth will be able to restore the hair, and to make it grow on a barren soil,* while in the other instance it will certainly grow again. Scars, for instance, formed after destruction of the whole corium—as those left after vaccination—wherein the hair-sacs are implanted, will remain bald for a whole lifetime, while after slight burns, or other insignificant injuries, whereby the epidermis only has been destroyed, the latter will be restored, and the hair, if lost, will grow again. Another instance is that in which the hair-sacs are still in existence, but insufficiently active ; here we can sometimes excite their activity by application of local remedies, of which we shall have to speak when treating of the diseases to which the hair is subject.

Concerning the number of hairs, Withof has undertaken to count them. The value of such an account is, of course, a relative one, the numbers being different on different heads. According to Withof, a square inch of a male, moderately covered with hair, contains:—On the head 293 hairs; on the chin 39; on the pubic region 34; on the fore-arm 23; on the back of the hand 19; and on the front of the thigh 13 hairs.

On the rapidity of growth of the hair, Berthold has communicated some curious facts. The hair of the head of ladies from sixteen to twenty-four years of age grows at the rate of seven lines a month. The growth of the hair of the beard is quicker the oftener it is cut; shaved every twelve hours, it would attain a length of from 5½ to 12 inches per annum; shaved every twenty-four hours, from 5 to 7½ inches; every thirty-six hours, from 4 to 6½ inches. It grows faster by one-sixteenth during the day than during the night, and in eighteen days in the summer 0·026 more than in eighteen days in the winter.

CHAPTER VI.

ABNORMAL GROWTH OF THE HAIR.

THE growth of hair in man is, as already mentioned, by no means confined to the head and a few other regions of the body, but extends over the whole surface of the skin.

In almost all animals we see the hair forming a fur, but in man it acquires on a few spots only a considerable length, and on the others remains very fine and minute, so as to be discovered only by careful searching.

This is the normal state. But abnormally the hair even in man may acquire a considerable length on such parts as generally remain hairless, and such an excessive growth may render the appearance of the skin similar to that of a fur.

Excessive growth of the hair in men may therefore occur in the following instances :—

1. Upon spots where the hair normally ex-

hibits a considerable length, the latter may increase in a more or less high degree.

2. Where the hair, in a normal state, remains so fine and minute as scarcely to be seen, it may grow to a considerable length and turn the skin totally or partly into a kind of fur.

3. Growth of hair may take place on certain regions of persons where normally none are to be found, as, for instance, beards of ladies and children.

Of all these different kinds, numbers of cases are on record of recent and ancient times.

The superfluous growth of the human hair may extend, as already stated, over the whole surface of the body, and is then technically termed " *Universal Hypertrichosis,*" or it may be seen only to extend over certain parts, in which case it is called " *Local Hypertrichosis ;*" the term Hypertrichosis being composed of two Greek words—namely, " hyper," signifying " *more than necessary,*" and " trichos," being the Greek word for " hair." Tamponette showed to Borrichius, who was a renowned physician, a new-born child, entirely covered with hair; and Thomas Ficinus, in his book on the influence of certain impressions of the mother on the fœtus, relates the case of a girl at her birth entirely covered with hair and a kind of bristles, from the mother's often beholding the picture of St. John the Baptist, hanging over her bedside, drawn in his hairy vesture. The cousin of Pope Nicholas III. is said to have given birth to a similar child, from her often beholding a bear in her crest. Zacutus Lusitanus has published the history of a girl three years old, who was regularly made, but possessed of a beard and covered with hair all over her body. Eble relates a case of a child born with a downy beard, from the fact of her mother having been frightened by her husband when he had just finished soaping his beard before shaving. Scalinger saw a Spanish boy totally covered with white hairs, who, therefore, was called by the French *Barbet*.

Bichat and Villermé, in 1808, at Poitiers, saw a child of six or eight years of age, exhibiting large dark spots all over his body, and covering about the third part of it, on which spots bristle-like hair grew. The 14th volume of Hufeland's Journal contains the case of a girl of fourteen years, whose back was entirely covered with long, fair, curly hair, perfectly resembling that of a calf. A most remarkable case has been published by Degner, concerning a girl who from the third year of her life began to be covered with hair at her back, abdomen, upper and lower extremities—the skin thus bearing a resemblance to that of a horse.

About 1830 a boy, three years old, named Stevenson, was living at Manor Gardens, Chelsea, one-half of whose body, from his birth, was covered with brownish hairs, resembling in thickness and colour those of his head. The skin on which these hairs grew was likewise of a brown hue, beginning at the hinder and lower part of the neck, extending over the back and the lower part of the abdomen, and totally covering the front and back parts of the thighs down to the knees.

There are many instances on record to show that the abnormal growth of the hair may as well be acquired by a hereditary taint as by disease; thus the hair of the once renowned dancer, Negreni, after her escape from an acute disease, grew to a length of over three yards, and many of us remember the Spanish dancer, Julia Pastrana, who was not only possessed of a fine beard, but whose whole body was hairy.

FIG. 8.

We give her photograph (fig. 8), and it may be mentioned that she had a child whose hair began to grow in a similar manner to that on the skin of his mother.

The phenomenon of excessive growth of the hair of the whole body having passed through three generations has been observed

in a family at Ava at different times and by
different reliable authorities.

It was John Crawford, who, in his " Journal
of an Embassy from the Governor-General of
India to the Court of Ava," forty years ago,
first gave a description of Shwe-Maon and his
daughter Maphoon. The family was seen again
in 1855 by Captain Henry Youle, who gave a
description of them in his " Narrative of the
Mission sent by the Governor-General of India
to the Court of Ava." And lastly, Maphoon
and her children were seen only a year ago
by Captain Houghton, who had photographs
taken from them, for copies of which I am
much indebted to the Rev. Mr. Houghton, of
Wellington, Salop, and to my friend, the Rev.
J. G. Wood, of Belvedere.

The case is so very rare and curious that
I need no apology for the reproduction of the
descriptions given by Crawford and Youle, nor
for giving the pictures and photographs of
all the members of that remarkable family.

Speaking of Shwe-Maon, Crawford says—
" We have heard much of a person said to
be covered all over with hair, and who, it was
insisted upon, more resembled an ape than a

human being—a description, however, I am glad to say, which was by no means realized by his appearance.

FIG. 9.*

" Having expressed a curiosity, to see this individual, the king politely sent him over to our dwelling, some days ago, and Dr. Wallich

---

* Fig. 9 is Shwe-Maon's portrait, photographically copied from Crawford's "Journal." Fig. 10 represents the profile somewhat larger.

and I took down on the spot the following account of himself, and this history. His name was Shwe-Maon, and he stated himself to be thirty years of age. He was a native of the district of Maeyong-gye, a country of Lao, situated on the Saluen, or Martaban river, three months' journey from Ava. Saubwa, as the chief of the country, presented him to the king as a curiosity when a child of five years of age, and he had remained in Ava ever since. His height was five feet three inches and a half, which is about the ordinary stature of the Burmese. His orm was slender, if compared with the usually robust make of the Hindoo-Chinese race, and his constitution was rather delicate. In his complexion there was nothing remarkable, although upon the whole he was rather fairer than the ordinary run of Burmese. The colour of his eyes was a dark brown, not so intense as that of the ordinary Burmese. The same thing may be said of the hair of the head, which was also a little finer in texture, and less copious.

" The whole forehead, the cheeks, the eyelids, the nose, including a portion of the inside, the chin—in short, the whole face, with the ex-

ception of the red portion of the lips—were
covered with a fine hair.   On the forehead
and cheeks this was eight inches long, and on
the nose and chin about four inches.   In
colour it was of a silvery grey; its texture
was silky, lank and straight.   The posterior
and inferior surface of the ears, with the
inside of the external ear, were completely
covered with hair of the same description as
that on the face, and about eight inches long:
it was this chiefly which contributed to give
his whole appearance at first sight an unnatural and almost inhuman aspect.   He may
be strictly said to have had neither eyelashes,
eyebrows, nor beard, or at least they were
supplanted by the same silky hair which enveloped the whole face.   He stated that,
when a child, the whole of this singular
covering was much fairer than at present.
The whole body, with the exception of the
hands and feet, was covered with hair of the
same texture and colour as that now described, but generally less abundant; it was
most plentiful over the spine and shoulders,
where it was five inches long; over the breast
it was about four inches; it was most scanty

on the bare arms, the legs, thighs, and abdomen. We thought it not improbable that this singular integument might be periodically or occasionally shed, and inquired, but there was no ground for this surmise — it was quite permanent.

Fig. 10.

" Although but thirty years of age, Shwe-Maon had, in some respects, the appearance of a man of fifty-five or sixty : this was owing to a singularity connected with the formation of the teeth, and the consequent falling in of the cheeks. On inspecting the mouth, it was discovered that he had in the lower jaw but five teeth—namely, the four incisors and the left canine ; and in the upper but four, the two outer ones of which partook of the canine form.   The molars or grinders were of course totally wanting.   The gums, where they should have been, were a hard fleshy ridge, and, judging from appearances, there was no alveolar process.   The few teeth he had were sound but rather small, and he had never lost any from disease.   He stated that he did not shed his infantile teeth till he was twenty years of age, when they were succeeded in the usual manner by the present set.   He also expressly asserted that he never had any molars, and that he experienced no inconvenience from the want of them.

" The features of this individual were regular and good for a Burmese.   The intellectual faculties were by no means deficient ; on the contrary, he was a person of very good sense, and his intelligence appeared to us to be rather above than below the ordinary Burmese standard.

" He gave the following account of the manner in which the hairy covering made its appearance.   At his birth his ears alone were covered with hair, about two inches long and of a flaxen colour.   At six years of age hair began to grow on the body generally, and first on the forehead. He distinctly stated that he did not attain the age of puberty till he was twenty years old.

"Shwe-Maon was married about eight years ago, or when twenty-two years of age, the king, as he stated himself, having made him a present of a wife. By this woman he has had four children, all girls; the eldest died when three years of age, and the second when eleven months old. There was nothing remarkable in their form. The mother, a rather pretty Burmese woman, came to us to-day along with the third and fourth child. The eldest, about five years of age, was a striking likeness of her mother, and a pretty, interesting child, without malformation whatever, or indeed anything to distinguish her from an ordinary healthy child. She began to teeth at the usual period, and had all her infantile teeth complete at two years of age. The youngest child was about two years and a half old, a very stout fine infant; she was born with hair in the interior portion of the ear. At six months old it began to appear all over the ears, and at one year old on different parts of the body. This hair was of a light flaxen colour, and of a fine silky texture. When two years of age, and not until then, she got a couple of incisor teeth in each jaw, but had as yet neither canine nor molar. Shwe-Maon assured us that none of his parents or relations, and as far as he knew, none of his countrymen, were marked like himself. Shwe-Maon, we found, had been occasionally employed by the Court as a buffoon, having been taught to imitate the antics of a monkey. For these feats, however, the poor fellow does not seem very liberally rewarded; for to subsist himself and family he was obliged to betake himself to the trade of basket-maker, in which he was now employed. He would have turned his monstrosity to better account in London."

Of Maphoon Captain Youle gives the following account :—

" The whole of Maphoon's face was more or less covered with hair. On a part of the cheek, and between the nose and mouth, this was confined to a short down, but over all the rest of the face was a thick silky hair of a brown colour, paleing about the nose and chin,

four or five inches long. At the alæ of the
nose, under the eye, and on the cheekbone
this was very fully developed; but it was in
and on the ear that it was most extraordinary.
Except the upper tip, no part of the ear was

FIG. 11.

visible. All the rest was filled and veiled with
a large mass of silky hair, growing apparently
out of every part of the external organ, and

hanging a pendant lock to a length of eight
or ten inches. The hair over her forehead
was brushed so as to blend with the hair of the
head, the latter being dressed (as usual with
her countrywomen) *à la Chinoise.* It was
not so thick as to conceal her forehead.

" The nose densely covered with hair, as no
animal's is that I know of, and with long locks
curving out and pendant like the wisps of a
fine Skye terrier's coat, had a most strange
appearance. The beard was pale in colour,
and about four inches in length, seemingly
very soft and silky.

" Poor Maphoon's manners were good and
modest, her voice soft and feminine, and her
expression mild and not unpleasing, after the
first instinctive repulsion was overcome. Her
appearance rather suggested the idea of a plea-
sant-looking woman masquerading, than that
of anything brutal. This discrimination was,
however, very difficult to preserve in sketching
her likeness, a task which devolved on me to-
day, in Mr. Grant's absence. On an after
visit, however, Mr. Grant made a portrait of
her, which was generally acknowledged to be
most successful.

" Her neck, bosom, and arms appeared to be covered with a fine pale down, scarcely visible in some lights. She made a move as if to take off her upper clothing, but reluctantly, and we prevented it. Her husband and two boys accompanied her. The elder boy, about four or five years old, had nothing

FIG. 12.

abnormal about him. The youngest, who was fourteen months old, and still at the breast, was evidently taking after his mother. There was little hair on the head, but the child's ear was full of long silky floss, and it could boast a moustache and beard of pale silky down that would have cheered the heart of many a cornet. In fact, the appearance of the child agrees almost exactly with what Mr. Crawford says of Maphoon herself as an infant.

" This child is thus the third in descent exhibiting this strange peculiarity, and in this third generation, as in the two preceding, this peculiarity has appeared only in one individual.

" Maphoon has the same dental peculiarity also that her father had—the absence of the canine teeth and grinders, the back part of the gums presenting merely a hard ridge. Still she chews pawn like her neighbours."

In respect to excessively long beards—in men as well as in women—a great many instances are likewise on record. At the Prince-court of Eidam a life-sized portrait of a carpenter is to be seen, who when working wore his beard in a bag, for if freely hanging down it reached not only to the ground, but was still considerably longer, measuring in its length nine feet.

In the times of the Turkish wars a Hungarian soldier is said to have been possessed of a beard so large as to cover his whole body. Bartholin relates the history of a wandering monk whose beard extended to the ground, and in Braunau, a little town in Germany, the grave of the mayor of that town—Hans Steininger—is to be seen, whose beard likewise hung down to the ground, and who, in 1572, lost his life in consequence of having forgotten to raise his beard when mounting a horse, whereby the former became entangled with the stirrup, and caused the loss of its owner's life.

Though the whole human body, as we have seen, is covered with hair, yet it is comparatively rare to see an excessive growth on other parts than the head, chin, eye-brows, and pubic region; on the latter the growth in rare exceptions beginning in the centre of the abdomen. I have seen a lady who exhibited an excessive growth of hair in both her ears, forming long curls, reaching to the shoulders, which could only be discovered and distinguished from the hair of the head, when particular attention was drawn to them. The hair within the nostrils may also become much prolonged, and though excessive growth

of the down is rare, yet the latter is likewise liable to prolongation, and then forms

FIG. 13.

the so-called hairy skin, of which we find an
instance recorded in the Bible.

Hildanus gives the description of a boy
covered all over with hair, and Thoresby, in
his "Topography of Leeds," relates the same
condition of a girl. Riolan, in his work "On
Monstrosities," gives the history of a hairy
man who was even mistaken for a bear ; and
Van Horne dissected the body of a certain
Martinez del Salper, who in a paroxysm of
ague had committed suicide, and whose
thorax, abdomen, back, and upper extremities
were entirely covered with hair, which on the

back exhibited, moreover, the peculiarity that the direction of the hair was not downwards but upwards. The shoulders were just like those of a bear.

In olden times, particularly in Greece, such hair-covered men were called " Satyrs," of whom Plutarch, Diodorus, Arrianus, Pomponius Mela, and many other authors, have given accounts.

A well-developed specimen of excessive growth of hair has recently been observed in the metropolis by Mr. Paget, and published in the *Lancet* of August, 1867.

The child represented in fig. 14 was admitted into St. Bartholomew's Hospital in 1865.

She was at that time twelve years old. The left upper extremity and the greater part of the corresponding side of the trunk and neck were deeply stained with dark brown pigment, from which grew an abundant crop of brown, harsh, lank hair, varying in length from one to two inches. The skin was rough and harsh; the arm was long, thin, and withered; the scapula was naturally prominent. In fact, the upper limb, shoulder, and back

G

bore a very strong resemblance to the corresponding parts of a monkey. The mother
stated that when three months pregnant with

FIG. 14.

the child she was much terrified by a monkey
attached to a street organ, which jumped on
her back as she was passing by.

In conclusion, attention must be drawn to

the relation which seems to exist between the abnormal growth of hair and the abnormal development of the teeth, as not only noticed in the hairy family at Ava, and in Julia Pastrana and her child, but as occurring also in animals. According to Mr. Darwin,* Mr. Yarrell found many of the teeth deficient in three hairless "Egyptian" dogs, and in a hairless terrier. The incisors, canines, and premolars suffered most, but in one case all the teeth, except the large tubercular molar on each side, were deficient. With men, continues Darwin, several striking cases have been recorded of inherited baldness, with inherited deficiency, either complete or partial, of the teeth. We see the same connexion in those rare cases in which the hair has been renewed in old age, for this has "usually been accompanied by a renewal of the teeth." After referring to the hairy family described above, and to the Spanish dancer, who had in both the upper and lower jaw an irregular double set of teeth, one row being placed within the other, and whose face, from the redundancy of the pro-

---

* "Animals and Plants under Domestication," vol. ii. p. 326.

jecting teeth, had a gorilla-like appearance, Mr. Darwin is of opinion that these cases and those of the hairless dogs forcibly call to mind the fact, that the two orders of mammals—namely, the edentata and cetacea—which are the most abnormal in their dermal covering, are likewise the most abnormal either by deficiency or redundancy of teeth.

From the time of the Greeks and Romans until now, authors have mentioned different tribes whom they described to be covered all over with hair, but as often as opportunity has been offered to examine the truth of such descriptions, they have been found void of foundation. Recently the inhabitants of Yesso have been described as hairy, and though these descriptions have been repeated by different writers, we must nevertheless hesitate in accepting them as true until still further confirmed by reliable travellers.

We extract the following from a paper read by Mr. W. Martin Wood at a meeting of the Ethnological Society of London, entitled " The Hairy Men of Yesso."*

---

* " Transactions of the Ethnological Society," 1866, vol. iv. p. 34.

" Yesso is the most northern portion of the empire of Japan. These aborigines are named 'Aïnos' or 'Mosinos'—the 'all hairy people,' —this last being a Japanese term which implies their chief physical peculiarity. Their number is estimated at about fifty thousand.

" The Aïnos live quite in the interior of the island, and seldom show themselves at Hako-dadi, or Mats-mai, two of the principal cities of the island, except when on their embassy in spring or in autumn, when they come to ex-change their dried fish and furs for rice and hunting-gear. Of a timid and shrinking de-portment, these people seem utterly crushed in spirit by their long subjection and isolation. They are short in stature, of thick-set figure, and clumsy in their movements. Their physical strength is considerable; but besides that pecu-liarity, there would seem to be nothing by which an observer can recognise the possibility of the Aïnos ever having possessed any military virtue. The uncouthness and wildness of their aspect is calculated at first to strike a stranger with dismay or repugnance. Esau himself could not have been a more hairy man than are these Aïnos. The hair on their heads forms an enormous bush, and it is thick and matted. Their beards are very thick and long, and the greater part of their face is covered with hair which is generally dark in colour; but they have prominent foreheads, and mild dark eyes, which somewhat relieve the savage aspect of their visage. Their hands and arms, and indeed the greater part of their bodies, are covered with an abnormal profusion of hair. The natural colour of their skins is somewhat paler than that of the Japanese, but it is browned by their constant exposure."

In order to show how contradictory the statements of travellers are, who have even been at Yesso and seen the inhabitants of that island, I quote Barnard Davis' account given in the third volume of the " Memoirs of the Anthropological Society of London :"—

" There are certain questions which deserve to be carefully examined. *The hairiness of the Aïnos* is one of them. They have had conferred upon them the name of 'the hairy men of Yesso,' and both Chinese and Japanese writers allude to this peculiarity. The Japanese represent them as barbarians in an eminent measure, and call them 'Morin,' explained by

Klaproth as ' Hairy bodies.' They have also
been named ' Hairy Kuriles.' Still, the more
instructed Japanese do the Aïnos greater
justice. In a drawing of an Aïno man made
by Syo-da Sabon-ro, English and French
interpreter of the Embassy of the Tycoon of
Japan to Paris, in 1864, he is represented as
having long straggling locks falling down on
each side of his head, and a rough beard of no
very unusual length. Captain Broughton,
whose voyage was from 1795 to 1798, reported
that their bodies were almost covered with long
black hair, and that the same was to be seen
in some young children. Von Krusenstern
testified, from an examination of some Aïnos
in the north of Yesso, that he found them,
with the exception of their bushy beards and
the hair on their faces, as smooth as other
people. In the great Bay or Gulf of Amiwa,
at the south of the Island of Saghalien, he
induced several to uncover their bodies, and
says, ' We were convinced to a certainty that
the greater part of the Aïnos have no more
hair on their bodies than is to be found on
those of many Europeans.' He speaks of
' the greater part,' because in Mordiomeff

Bay he had met with a child only eight years old, with his body entirely covered with hair, although his parents and several other adult persons in the same place were not more hairy than Europeans. Hence Von Krusenstern declares the extreme hairiness of the Aïnos to be a fable, or exaggerated. Such is also the testimony of Lieutenant A. W. Habersham, of the U. S. Navy. His account is deserving of quotation at length. 'The hairy endowments of these people are by no means so extensive as some early writers lead one to suppose. As a general rule, they shave the front of the head *à la Japonnaise*, and though the remaining hair is undoubtedly very thick and coarse, yet it is also very straight, and owes its bushy appearance to the simple fact of constant scratching and seldom combing. The remaining hair they part in the middle, and allow to grow within an inch of the shoulder. The prevailing hue is black, but it often possesses a brownish cast, and these exceptions cannot be owing to the sun, as it is but reasonable to suppose that they suffer a like exposure from infancy up. Like the hair, their beard is bushy, and from the same causes. It is generally black, but often brownish, and seldom exceeds five or six inches in length. I only saw one case where it reached more than half way to the waist; and here the owner was evidently proud of its great length, as he had it twisted into innumerable small ringlets, well greased, and kept in something like order. His *hair*, however, was as bushy as that of any other. As this individual was evidently the most 'hairy Kurile' of the party, we selected him as the one most likely to substantiate the assertion of Broughton in regard to 'their bodies being almost universally covered with long black hair.' He readily bared his arms and shoulders for inspection, and (if I except a tuft of hair on each shoulder-blade, of the size of one's hand) we found his body to be no more hairy than that of several of our own men. The existence of these two tufts of hair caused us to examine several others, which examination established his as an isolated case."*

This fully confirms the statement of Von Krusenstern. " They wear the hair of their

---

* Nott and Gliddon's " Indigenous Races of the Earth," 1857, p. 620.

heads and their beards, usually their only covering to this part of their bodies, long and flowing, as a defence against the climate in which they dwell, which at certain seasons is sufficiently severe ; and it is probable that at times they are unusually hairy."

CHAPTER VII.

WE have seen in a previous chapter that the colour of the hair depends on three conditions, viz. :—

1. *The colour* of the cortical cells, which plays the most important part, and varies from very light yellow, through intense red, and all shades of brown, to a deep, dark hue, as seen in the hair of the negro.

2. *The molecules, consisting of pigment,* diffused through the cells of the cortical substance. It is diminished in fair, and entirely absent in grey and white hair, in which the colouring matter of the cells may likewise have—though not necessarily—disappeared.

3. *The amount of air contained both in the air cavities and the medullary canal.*—It is only recently that the part of the air contained in hairs has been more carefully investigated

and recognised. About twenty years ago a case was observed by Professors Schultze and Baum at Greifswald, concerning a healthy youth, sixteen years of age, whose hairs were coloured in such a manner as to form rings, alternately coloured white and brown. This state, giving to the head a grey appearance, was recognised as dependent upon an abnormal amount of air which had entered into the medullary tube. This case was published by Professor Karsch. The second case, of quite a similar nature, was, remarkably enough, observed in 1866, in the same city, by Dr. Landois. In this instance the hair became *grey* in the course of a few days; and we may suppose that in most cases in which the colour of the hair was turned grey in a few days, nay, in a few hours (many well-observed cases are on record) the same process has taken place as that described by Dr. Landois. He observed under the microscope the white spots to be filled with minute air-vesicles, whilst the pigment could be seen well-preserved in all parts of the hair. Here we have an instance in which the hair was grey, notwithstanding the cortical cells were naturally-coloured. The air-vesicles were not only confined to the medullary canal, but the cortical substance was likewise perfectly filled with them.

Dr. Landois is of opinion that the air-vesicles did not enter the hair from without, but were developed within. That such may be the case I shall be able to show when treating of inflation and cracking of the hairs.

The third case was observed by Erasmus Wilson, and read at a meeting of the Royal Society in March, 1867 :—" The hair was taken from a delicate but otherwise healthy boy, aged seven years and a half, a gentleman's son. Every hair of his head is brown and white in alternate bands, looking as if encircled with rings, and this change of aspect extends throughout the whole length of the hair, and gives to the general mass a curiously speckled character. The brown segment of the hair, which represents its normal colour, measures about one-fiftieth of an inch, and the two together about one thirty-sixth of an inch, or one-third of a line.

" Examination of the hair with a lens shows that the cylinder of the hair is perfectly uniform ; that the white portion is contained within the cuticle, and occupies the whole breadth of the cylinder; whilst it frequently presents a rounded cone at the central extremity, and breaks up into fibres at the opposite or distal end; and in some instances this fibrous structure is apparent at both ends of the white segment. Moreover, by transmitted light, the white segment is found to be opaque, and consequently presents a dark shade, while the intermediate or brown portion has the transparency of normal hair.

" When the transparency of the hair is increased by immersion in Canada balsam slightly diluted with spirits of turpentine, the white and opaque segment is reduced in dimensions, and is rendered more or less transparent by imbibition of the volatile fluid. Moreover, it is clearly demonstrated by this process, that the opacity of the segment, its whiteness when seen by reflected light, and its darkness by transmitted light, are all due to the presence of spaces in the fibrous portion of the hair, filled with air-globules. The air-spaces are necessarily very numerous and assembled closely together, while at the ends of the white segment they have more or less of a linear arrangement, and give a fibrous

appearance to the opaque mass. Moreover,
the partial transparency of the hair caused by
the balsam demonstrates that, besides the air-
spaces, large and small, contained in the
opaque portion, minute air-spaces, sometimes
arranged in linear order, and sometimes com-
municating and forming short, irregular canals,
are also met with in the transparent part of
the hair. And in addition to the minute air-
spaces of the plates of the fibrous portion of
the hair, an accumulation of air-globules is
also very apparent in the cells of the medulla.

"It is evident from this examination of
the hairs, that they are imperfect in structure and development, and that their imper-
fection indicates a weak producing organ, and
probably a weakly constitution of the indi- '
vidual; that the cells of which the fibrous
portion of the hair is composed, instead of
being filled with a horny plasma, are tinged
with aqueous fluid, and the desiccation of this
fluid leaves behind it vacuities which, in the
subsequent growth of the shaft, become filled
with air. The most remarkable phenomenon
in connexion with the case, however, is the
alternation of imperfect and perfect cells;

the period of continuance of the two processes, supposing them to be equally active in
point of time, being twice as long for the
perfect as for the imperfect structure.

" Since the publication of the observations
of Berthold in Müller's *Archiv* for 1850, it is
generally believed that the hair grows faster
during the day than during the night. Hence
the first suggestion that occurred to me in
connexion with the present case, seeing that
the white or opaque segment was shorter by
one-half than the brown, was that the former
represented the slower growth by night, and
the latter the quicker growth by day; the
white and the brown together representing an
entire day of twenty-four hours. But other
observations by myself have given, as the
average growth of the hair of the head in
persons who had been shaved, one-eighth of
an inch for the week, and consequently one
fifty-sixth of an inch for the twenty-four
hours. Now, the length of hair compre-
hended by the white and the brown in the
present case is one thirty-sixth of an inch,
and consequently a much more active growth
than is normally met with, corresponding, in

fact, in a similar ratio, with thirty-seven hours instead of twenty-four.

" I therefore refrain from speculating upon the cause of alternation of the healthy and morbid structure presented by this case, and restrict myself to the narration of the fact that, during a certain space of time, amounting to a day or more, the hair is produced of normal structure; while during another space of time, of undetermined extent, the hair is produced unhealthily; that the periods of healthy formation correspond pretty accurately in extent, as do those of unhealthy formation; while the latter in measurement are only half as extensive as the former; moreover, that the differences of the pathological operation are the production of a horny plasma in the normal process, and of serous and watery cell-contents in the abnormal process.

" I may further observe, that it is by no means improbable that the ' dead' and faded hair which is met with after some illnesses, and in instances of debilitated health, may be due to a similar pathological process, although wanting in the periodicity and alternation which render the present case so remarkable."

From what we have said of the colour of the
human hair it is quite evident that a yellow,
blue, or green hue is not met with in a normal
state of the human hair.   But, nevertheless,
such colours have been described by several
authors as occurring in the hair of man; at
times when the knowledge of physiological processes was rather curious, and when authors
imagined they had acquired the clue to any
phenomenon when they were in possession of
a mere word for the same, such descriptions
have been given without examination of their
true value.

"Certain humours of the body," says Bar-
tholinus, " as, for instance, the bile, are green,
why should the excrements of these humours,
as the hair, not be of the same hue ?"

Riedlin describes yellow hair, but his case
was not a physiological one, the person being
a patient suffering from jaundice, and Riedlin's
remarks are so very short, that it is impossible
to arrive at a certain conclusion in respect to
the colour of his patient's hair.

Green hair has been observed by many
authors, but in persons only who have been
working in copper mines or in copper factories.

Borillus describes an excitable friend of his who used to shed bloody tears when in passion, and mentions a medical student whose perspiration was of a green colour. "There is, therefore," continues Borillus, "nothing extraordinary in the hair also being green tinged, as I have recently seen in a youth."

Peter Frank likewise relates some instances of green hair in persons engaged in copper mines.

Eble, the author of a voluminous book on hair in the animal and vegetable kingdom, on this subject refers but to observations of others, and sums up his remarks thus:—"Blue and green hair are generally ascribed to the metallic evaporations of certain mines, and the occurrence of such coloured hair in a normal state has generally been denied. In such instances, of course, experience alone can be decisive, and since I have myself never been fortunate enough to see a person with blue or green hair, I must leave it to the reader whether he chooses to believe in the abnormity or not."

Dr. Rommel, when a student in Italy, saw at Padua a peasant thirty years of age, whose hair was entirely green, though he had never been engaged in metal works, nor applied anything to his hair.

According to Borillus, the labourers in copper mines or copper factories are distinguished by green hair, those of cobalt mines by blue hair; the workmen of brass-factories, particularly such as are engaged in pointing needles, by bluish or greenish hair. It is necessary to know, says Eble, that the colour in these workmen is not merely superficial, but penetrates the whole substance of the hair in such a manner as not to be wiped off the hair's surface.

According to the opinion of almost all observers to whom I have just referred, it seems to be an acknowledged fact, that the abnormal colour of hair occasionally met with, as for instance green, blue, yellow, &c., is not natural, but artificial, and that the occurrence of that abnormal colour is limited to labourers in certain mines and factories, and that even in these persons it is rare.

But, notwithstanding these facts, the cases when met with are of interest, and the unaccustomed aspect of a head perfectly blue, at

first sight astonishes the observer in a high
degree.

Having recently had an opportunity of ob-
serving a man adorned with blue hair, and
not finding that a microscopic examination
of hair, abnormally coloured, has ever been
published, I give in the following woodcut a
fair representation of a blue hair, as taken
from the man just mentioned.

The hair was taken from a patient under
my care in the Metropolitan Free Hospital.
He was a labourer in an indigo warehouse,
fifty-eight years of age, and not suffering from
any serious illness. On his entrance into my
consulting room, my attention was at once
drawn to the peculiar dark blue colour of the
hair of his head. John Borne—that was the
name of the patient—has been employed for
the last twenty-five years in his present
position; the peculiar hue of his hair he
noticed about twenty years ago; he never
neglected to brush his head daily, and to wash
it now and then, whereby the water became
slightly blue coloured, without altering the
colour of the hair.

With his consent, I clipped a quantity off

FIG. 15.

his head for my collection and for examination.

The microscope revealed the appearances illustrated in the opposite woodcut. They are easily intelligible without long comment. The hair is not uniformly coloured, as if dyed, but on its surface small particles of indigo are more or less firmly attached to it, whereby the whole mass of hair assumes an appearance as if it were uniformly blue coloured ; the indigo particles could, by means of a knife, be scraped off the hair, which remained grey, the natural colour of Borne's head. The contrast of the grey, or rather white hair, and the dark blue indigo particles, gave a handsome picture under the microscope, and as, besides the indigo particles, a very fine dust of the same substance was attached to the lines formed by the cells of the cuticle of the hair, these lines were hereby much more marked than is the case in normal hair.

Some of the hairs were partly or totally wrapped in an indigo crust ; others were glued together by means of the colouring matter, which did not penetrate into the substance of the hair. Whether the appearance of the

hair of labourers in mines or factories is different from that just described—viz., whether
certain oxides of metals are formed on the
surface of their hair in such a manner as to
combine with the hair substance as certain
hair dyes do, is not known, since—with the
exception of Eble's short remark—no writer
has entered upon the subject.

CHAPTER VIII.

It has been a matter of long discussion whether or not such parts of the body as are not immediately connected with and influenced by nerves and bloodvessels are liable to disease; the epidermis, the nails, and the hair are such parts of the human body.

There can be no question that the hair—which concerns us at present—participates in diseases of the body; it loses its glossy appearance, becomes brittle, inflated, and altered in many respects, or alters its colour under certain circumstances. Now if disease is the tendency of an organ or part of the human frame to deviate from its physiological—that is, the normal line of life, I do not see any reason why we should not call alterations occurring in the normal growth or structure of the hair " disease."

But all this refers only to the shaft of the hair, for its root being closely enveloped in the hair-sac, which is largely supplied with

nerves and vessels, undergoes many pathological alterations. To these is due the fall-
ing-off of the hair, which may be the result of
total destruction of the hair-sac, or of the
bulb only; in the former instance, permanent
baldness is the result, the skin assuming the
well-known glossy appearance known under
the popular term of "moonshine," while in
loss of hair, without destruction of the hair-
sac, occurring after serious illnesses—typhus
fever, for instance—growth may take place
again. But under such altered conditions,
the production of hair substance and colouring matter may be increased, so that the hair
may not only grow denser, but at the same
time be of an altered, generally of a darker
colour than before the illness, so that a fair lady
may become adorned with dark-coloured hair.

There are, therefore, diseases concerning the
hair shaft only, and affections concerning the
root of the hair alone, or the root and shaft
together.

To the diseases of the former kind apply the
remarks which we have made in a previous
chapter concerning the bleaching of the hair.

We have seen that this alteration may be

the result of air entering the tissue of the hair, an affection which from a certain point of view may be compared to an abnormal state of the connective-tissue, likewise produced by air, which, under certain circumstances, enters through a wound or otherwise, and is called " Emphysema."

The first instance of an altered condition of the hair-tissue arising from within the hair, and causing alterations both in the shape and firmness of the hair, was published by myself in 1855, in the " Transactions of the Academy of Vienna," vol. xvii. p. 612.

The disease which I have called "*Inflation and cracking of the hair*," is illustrated in the following woodcut, and has also been observed by Erasmus Wilson.

The hair of the beard of the gentleman in whom I first noticed the affection, was marked by minute white points, from two to seven and even more in one shaft. At first sight these points made the impression of nits, but on traction the hair easily broke off at one of these little white spots, and when put under the microscope, had the appearance seen in fig. 16.

FIG. 16.

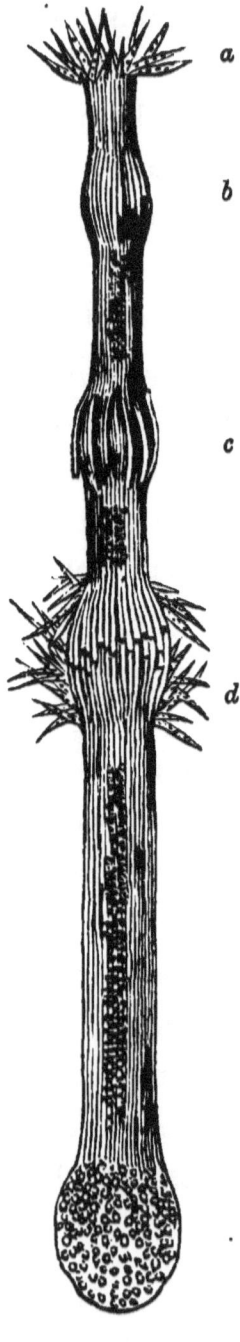

The figure shows one such hair in different stages of disease. At *b* we see a mere bulbiform alteration of the hair; at *c*, a more advanced stage, the bulb not only being larger, but parts of the cuticle being separated unmistakeably by a pressure from within to which they could offer no sufficient resistance. This internal pressure seems to have been still greater at *d*, so as to cause the whole circumference of the hair to burst, the broken spot resembling two outspread brushes, meeting each other by their ends. On traction such a spot breaks off, leaving particles of the cuticle and cortical substance as seen at *a*. Wilson is of opinion than this affection originates, like other defects of structure, in nutritive debility. A physician, who consulted him for this state of hair informed him that it began while he was pursuing his studies at Edinburgh, that he recovered during a short residence in Australia, but that it re-appeared on his return to Scotland.

The two gentlemen in whom I have observed the alteration in question were strong and well-nourished; the growth of their hair was dense, but nevertheless a defective nutritive condition may have existed in their hair. For there is no other explanation of the phenomena just described than that of certain gases having originated within the substance of the hair, and exercising a pressure from within, first gave rise to the bulbiform shape, which ultimately resulted in the cracking of the whole circumference of the hair's substance.

This opinion gains strength by the fact of the medullary canal being deficient at those spots which have been cracked.

It need not be remarked that hair affected in such a manner cannot be reinstalled in its former state. Neither application of lotions nor other remedies will be of any avail. If the affection exists in a slight or moderate degree, no interference is necessary, but when to a great extent, so as to be disagreeable by the mere aspect, the best advice is to have the beard shaved, which must be repeated at intervals should the affection recur.

In conclusion, it may be stated that only a few such cases have been observed by Erasmus Wilson and myself, and the gentlemen who were the subjects of my observation exhibited the disease in their moustaches and beards; I have not observed it in the hair of the head.

CHAPTER IX.

BEFORE the time when the chignon question was discussed in the daily papers, the term " gregarine," I suppose, was known to those only who had made lower animal life their special study, and the question therefore naturally arose, What is a gregarine?

A gregarine is one of those beings which stand at the point where the vegetable kingdom terminates and the animal begins. It is therefore but natural that some observers look at gregarines as vegetable growths, while others claim them as lower animals, consisting only of one or of a few cells which multiply by division. There are many different kinds of gregarines, one of which you may readily see if you put the contents of the intestines of a common black-beetle under the microscope.

It must be mentioned that other minute growths, of the vegetable nature of which there is not the slightest doubt, consisting also of one or of a few cells only, resemble gregarines very closely.

Now, in 1866, Professor Lindemann of Petersburgh published some observations of what he considered "gregarines," found by him in artificial hair.   The observations gave rise to a kind of panic, as well amongst the manufacturers as amongst the fair wearers of chignons.

The question was taken up rather by the daily papers than by scientific journals; and incompetent observers, who were not accustomed to microscopic work, soon confirmed Professor Lindemann's observations.

It was just at that time when an opportunity was offered to me of examining a great number of samples of hair, amongst which one sample came from the premises of Messrs. Hovenden and Sons, of City-road, who deal largely in artificial hair.   This sample gave full explanation of what Lindemann had seen.

The "head of hair" from which the sample in question had been taken, was laid aside by the workmen employed in Messrs. Hovenden's workshop as totally unfit for being cleaned, each hair exhibiting a number of knots, which by the usual very perfect cleaning process could not be separated. The hair substance itself was not broken, as was the case in the

FIG. 17.

I

hair described in the previous chapter, but proved firm on traction. On close examination each knot could be seen forming a sheath round the hair, and with some precaution could be wholly abstracted from it.

Fig. 17 shows the appearance of the hair under the microscope, which at once revealed the knots to consist of some cellular masses.

On preparing such a knot for microscopic examination, so as to form a thin layer, and viewing it under a high power, I could see what is represented in fig. 18.

Fig. 18.

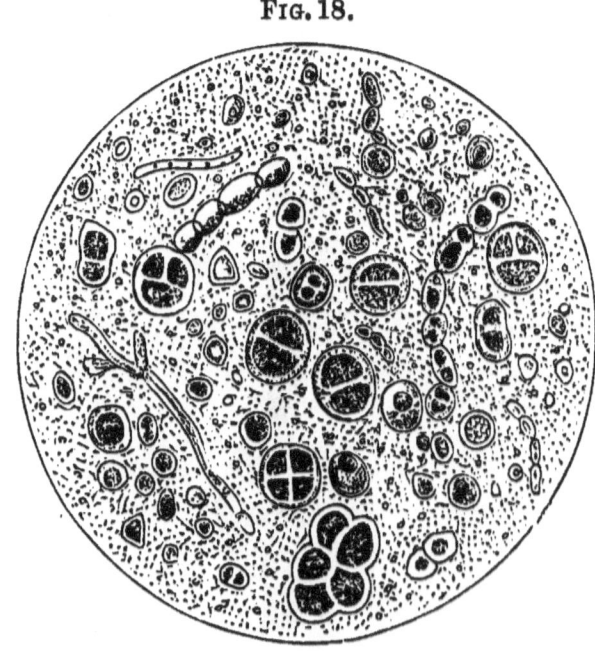

The woodcut shows, besides chains which are easily recognisable as belonging to the vegetable kingdom, large round cells, containing two or four (sometimes three) large nuclei. These cells resemble, in fact, gregarines, and it may be mentioned that several first-rate observers, to whom I have sent samples of the hair, were at first sight of opinion that they had Lindemann's gregarines under the microscope, but closer examination soon showed this assumption to be erroneous.

Dr. Küchenmeister of Dresden, whom I consulted about the nature of what I had recognised as a fungus, asked the opinion of Professor Rabenhorst of Dresden, one of the greatest continental authorities on microscopic fungi. Both authorities pronounced the fungus to be a new species of *pleurococcus*, and did me the honour of applying my name to it, and, therefore, calling it *Pleurococcus Beigeli*.

Comparing this fungus with the beings described by Lindemann, there remained not the slightest doubt that this gentleman had seen the fungus just mentioned and mistaken it for gregarines. A practical question now arose—namely, whether or not the assertion of some observers be true, that the growths, be they vegetable or animal, when in contact with the human skin, produce a diseased state of that organ.

This question has been satisfactorily settled by me, as will be seen hereafter.

Gregarines, if placed in a saccharine solution, or in such other conditions as make vegetables grow, never alter their shape or structure, propagating by division, and never giving rise to such alterations as microscopic fungi do, which may at once be recognised as such.

The nodes of the hair form dirty brownish thickenings; if moistened with water they are easily removable. The single cells are mostly round, and at the time of partition as large as $\frac{1}{300}$th part of a line. After partition the young cells very soon attain the size of $\frac{1}{650}$th part of a line in diameter. They are transparent, and of a light green colour. They are united in groups, and involved in a rather thickish transparent green mucus. The cell-membrane is so thick as distinctly to show a double contour, but no layers are visible.   It is homogeneous, and of light appearance like glass.

These cells, when put into a saccharine solution and exposed to a moderate temperature, soon alter their shape, and begin to grow very rapidly.   After a few hours, when viewed under the microscope, the large nuclei are seen free from their common enveloping membrane, and each nucleus becoming an independent cell, containing one, two, or more nuclei and nucleoli, as seen in fig. 19.

FIG. 19.

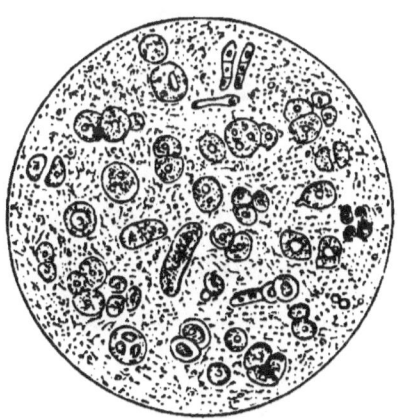

If the process of development be carried on longer, they go through a number of stages, and after about thirty or forty hours large ramifications may be seen, and likewise the reproduction of the original form of the fungus may be observed, as seen in fig. 20.

FIG. 20.

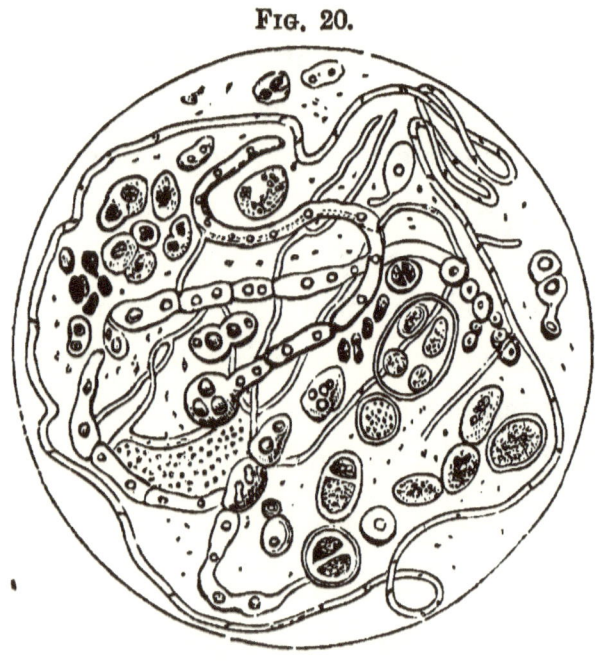

All these different stages have not only been produced and observed by me in saccharine and other solutions, but the fungus has likewise flourished for more than a fortnight on my arm, which was blistered before the fungus had been transplanted to it; and though the growth had taken place with great rapidity, yet it has not only produced no ill-effect on the skin, but the blistered place healed up during the growth of fungus on it.

All statements which have been made in respect to the danger of the "gregarines of the chignons" have therefore been mere consequences of gross ignorance or imperfect observation.

Firstly, because Lindemann's gregarines were no gregarines, but fungi.

Secondly, because these fungi are not only not peculiar to chignons, but the hair on which they are met with is—as in our case—totally unfit for the manufacture of chignons.

Thirdly, because not the slightest affection would or could be produced on the skin, if by some chance such a fungus should come into contact with the body.   For if it was not able to produce any alteration on the skin deprived of its cuticle, it would certainly still less influence the skin with the epidermis intact.

In order to have the opinion of the highest authority I sent some specimens to Professor Hallier of Jena, who for the last few years has been engaged in investigating the microscopic vegetable growths.   The results at which this observer arrived were so very remarkable that they have produced an entire revolution in our views concerning those

minute beings to which our fungus belongs.
Dr. Hallier has not only shown that in the
evacuations of cholera patients and of patients
suffering from typhus fever peculiar fungi
are to be found in innumerable quantities,
but that the effect of the lymph used for
vaccination depends on the presence of such

FIG. 21.

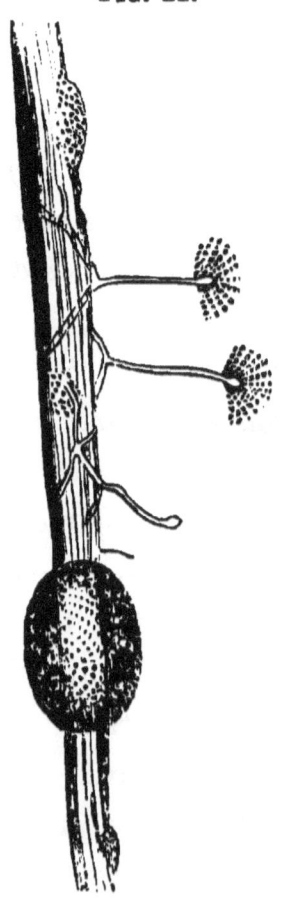

fungi, and that they are likewise present in measles, scarlatina, and other exanthematous diseases. Though Dr. Hallier's views have yet to undergo the clinical test before being generally adopted, yet it must already be acknowledged that the results of his researches are of the utmost importance.

According to Dr. Hallier, no fungus can be recognised as to the species to which it belongs, before having germinated and been carried through different generations, until its original form has been reproduced; for different stages of development of one and the same fungus may be so very dissimilar to the original fungus, that up to the present time they have been taken for separate species. Consequently Professor Hallier has considerably reduced the number of microscopic fungi, and has shown that many forms hitherto recognised as peculiar species were nothing but different stages, dependent on certain conditions of development of certain fungi, which can be reproduced when the development is carried on.

By this method Professor Hallier has formed the diagnosis of my fungus, differing from that of Drs. Küchenmeister and Rabenhorst.

According to Hallier, the fungus is a new species of *Sclerotium,* belonging to the mould kind, to which he gave the name of *Sclerotium Beigelianum.* Besides the fungus just mentioned, Aspergillus—another kind of microscopic growth—is found in the nodes on the hair.

Sclerotium is likewise but a stage of a well-known fungus, Penicillium, which has really been developed by Prof. Hallier on one of the hairs sent to him, and fig. 21 represents that hair, Penicillium reproduced on it from Sclerotium.

CHAPTER X.

In May, 1868, some hair of a lady was sent to me by a well-known hairdresser, asking me for an explanation of some peculiar appearances in the growth of the hair. The case was this:—The lady had well-grown, dense, and in all respects healthy and well-developed hair, on the shaft of which large numbers of whitish knots were visible, sometimes disappearing, but returning again and remaining for a considerable time. Their existence was rather disagreeable, inasmuch as the white knots could easily be mistaken for nits. The lady paid very great attention to the management of her hair, but in spite of the application of several lotions she was not able to prevent the recurrence of the disagreeable appearance.

Having been supplied with several samples of the hair, the first thing which I could make out by the naked eye was that the hair itself was not diseased, but that the formation of the knots or sheath round it had either taken place within the hair-sac, or that it was dependent upon circumstances not at all connected with the hair. When the latter was put under the microscope one could decide at the first glance that these knots were totally different from those described in the previous chapter, and the following woodcut is a fair representation of both the hair and knot, as seen under a low magnifying power.

The hair appears perfectly intact and normal in texture, but imbedded in a white, transparent, apparently structureless formation, of a very peculiar nature. The knots are large enough to be seen by the naked eye, some measuring a tenth part of a line in length. They adhere by no means firmly to the hair, but are rather loosely attached to it, and may be stripped off very easily. Under the microscope their formation in regular layers, something like the slates of a roof, is very striking. Although some of the divisions are a little narrower than others, yet the whole formation gives the impression of great regularity. There appears to be, as already mentioned, no particular structure, the stratum being only finely dotted, and here and there shrivelled. This is when a low power is used. But on applying a higher power to one of these knots, prepared for microscopic examination by application of water or glycerine, and exercising some pressure on the covering glass, in order to produce a very thin layer, a structure of a very well-known kind becomes visible. The whole knot, thus prepared, is found to consist of cells, identical with those of the inner transparent layer of the root sheath (see Chapter V.).

Finding these cells, the length of which corresponds with the divisions or partitions observable in the knot, and illustrated in the ac-

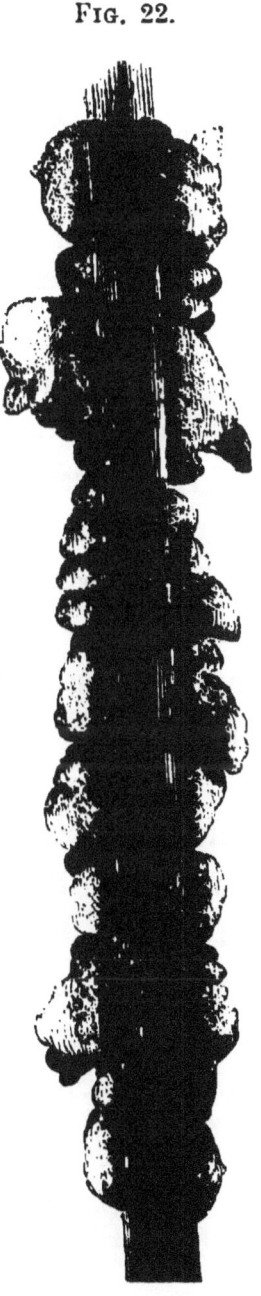

Fig. 22.

companying woodcut (fig. 22,) there remains no other explanation but the one, that a hyperplastic action—perhaps consequent on irritation or inflammation—exists in the sheaths of the roots of the hair, producing an abnormal number of cells, which are glued together and adhere to the cuticle of the hair while passing through the hair-sac. This affection, as far as I am aware, has never been observed before.

If the view in respect to the origin of these knots be correct, the advice to be given in this case would necessarily be such as to get rid of the knots already formed, and to prevent the abundant formation of new cells. To arrive at the first-mentioned end, it would be necessary to keep the hair well greased or oiled, and to comb it often with a very fine comb; for the latter purpose the application of some astringent lotion would be required, as, for instance, tannin, about two or three grains dissolved in an ounce of water, or sulphate of zinc of the same strength.

CHAPTER XI.

THERE is a disease of a most remarkable kind, the most prominent and most curious phenomenon of which consists in a matted state of the patient's hair. This disease is called *Plica polonica,* and occurs particularly in those countries inhabited by the Sclavonian race.

The aspect of a patient labouring under this disorder is, particularly if the plica be in an advanced stage, frightful. The disorder generally begins with most troublesome symptoms—affections of the head, eyes, skin, &c., increasing until the hair is either simply glued together and turned into a perfectly felty mass, or growing in enormous quantities, sometimes to an extraordinary length, and then becoming plaited and matted. If the latter be the case, the plica has been called by French writers "*Plique en queue,*" whilst to a plica which assumes the shape of a cap they give the name

"*Plique en masse.*"　Another form is that in which the head is covered with curls, each curl forming a separate small plica; this kind is known under the name of "*Caput Medusæ.*"

The disease does not affect men only, but the domestic animals also, the cattle, dog, pig, and cat; and it is a popular, although erroneous belief, in the countries where plica is endemic, that, when untangled or clipped, it is followed by most serious symptoms.

It is of very great interest to know that Shakspeare was familiar with the disease, as well as with the circumstances just alluded to, and it is therefore not impossible that the affection, in his time, was not rare in this country. At least we find in "Romeo and Juliet" (act i. scene 4)—

"This is that very Mab
That plaits the manes of horses in the night;
And bakes the elf-locks in foul sluttish hairs.
Which once untangled, much misfortune bodes."

Of recorded cases of plica polonica, observed in England, we know only two instances, which are interesting enough to be briefly related in this place. The one case was observed in the middle of the last century, and the second in 1866 by myself. In the "Philosophical Transactions" of May 28th, 1747, a letter was published by J. Amos, secretary of the Royal Society, directed to C. Mortimer, M.D., running thus :—

"Good Sir, — June 22nd, 1746, in the morning, Mrs. Hannah Coomes, a neat old woman, whose hair (of plica polonica, as it is called) I showed to the Society last Thursday, came and gave me the following information : —That she was of a gentle family in Staffordshire, who had suffered much in the civil war, and that her mother had her hair grown in the same manner, whose maiden name was Alice Goldsmith, but her own maiden name was Hannah Bundley, born in the Haymarket, in the Whitechapel, and baptized in Aldgate on a Saturday in June, 1675. Her mother having such short hair, used to comb *hers* much to prevent it, till sometimes the blood came. When she was about fourteen years old, she perceived it to grow thick, just about the back part of her head, and at length it grew to this matted long substance I now see it, of 109 inches long. She says she has had four husbands ; the first, Nicholas Woodcock, to whom she was married when about twenty-

K

eight years old, and had four children by him; all died young, but observed nothing of their hair growing so.

"I am, Sir, your obedient servant,

"J. AMES."

The second case which occurred in England was recorded by myself under the following circumstances:—In the daily papers of November 8th, 1866, a "horrible disclosure of misery" was published concerning a woman, Jane Mitchell, thirty-nine years old, of High Road Well, about a mile from Halifax, who had been discovered by the police. "The spectacle," says the report, "was most disgusting and appalling. Not an article of furniture was to be seen in the chamber, except a dark screen before the window. The floor was in some places more than an inch thick in dirt, potato parings, animal refuse, woollen flocks, &c. He (the policeman) next proceeded to remove the screen, and was appalled to find a human being huddled up in a lump, upon an old bed laid upon a wooden trunk, the whole being with dirt as black as a chimney-hole. Her hair was matted, and her whole appearance that of wretchedness and squalor. She was not lying, but rather reclining, or huddled with her back against a pillow. The whole place she occupied behind the screen was only three or four feet by half a yard broad. When the curtain was drawn aside she blasphemed, and wanted to know if the policeman had come to kill her. The sight was horrible. She refused to be removed or touched. At her right hand was a small darkened window, the recess of which was filled with vileness. Since the discovery, the sister, Eliza, has informed a neighbour that it is three years since her sister was washed, or had combed her hair, or had any chemise on. She had at present nothing on but a pair of old stockings, which had not been changed for years. Eliza stated her sister to be suffering from bodily debility, not insanity."

Having read this report, I wrote to Dr. Alexander of Halifax, asking him whether he knew anything about the case, as, if there existed anything like artificial plica polonica, it should be found on the head of this unfortunate woman.

My presumption was correct, and Dr. Alexander has been so kind as to send me two specimens of plica, accompanied by the following letter :—

" DEAR SIR,—I cut the hair from the head myself, and might have had any quantity, since I recommended the head to be shaved, as the only means of operating upon the agglutinated mass, and cleansing the scalp. The back hair was turned up into a knob as usual, and one sample sent you was at the end of it. It is evident, not being done in ringlets, that it could not separately be plaited in single plaits, like the loose end. All was matted and encrusted.—Yours, very truly,

WM. ALEXANDER, M.D.

" Dr. Beigel."

When I exhibited some of the plicas in my possession to the Pathological Society of London at their meeting on April 17th, 1866, a committee was formed, consisting of Dr. Cobbold, Mr. Jonathan Hutchinson, and myself, in order to examine the hair microscopically. The report of the committee was read at the following meeting of the Society, and has been published in vol. xvii. of the Pathological Society's Transactions.

CHAPTER XII.

A DISEASE which is very commonly met with is that generally called "baldness"—*alopecia.* It occurs in several different degrees, and may consist of the hair simply becoming thinner, or total loss of it on a limited spot—known as Area; or of loss of the hair over the whole scalp. In the first of these three conditions, one merely notices the hair becoming thin, and generally a larger quantity remaining in the comb when dressing, than is normally the case. In the second form a small spot is noticed which is deprived of its hair, and sometimes rapidly increasing, extends over the whole scalp. The hair sometimes does not fall out, but breaks off immediately above the skin; at other times other bald spots are forming while the first is increasing, and either remain separate or become confluent. Such separate spots have usually a perfectly circular shape, and besides some remnants of the former hair, a new down is visible. If such spots become again covered with hair, this is not by the old stumps growing or becoming longer, but by an entirely new formation of hair.

The stumps consist of the root of the hair, which wastes at a very early stage, becomes loosened, and therefore may be easily drawn out by slight traction. In the course of the disease the old stumps are pushed forwards by the newly-formed hair, or by fungi growing within and around the root of the hair.

At the beginning of the process, however, the surface is smooth, white, as if polished, and, according to some authors, less sensitive. It appears as if the normal functions had ceased at the diseased part, that circulation has become disturbed, and the action of the nerves altered. The whole process has the aspect of a nervous disease, in consequence of which shedding of the hair takes place. Some have even observed baldness following the course of certain nerves. The scalp is generally the place where this affection occurs, but baldness is by no means limited to that region, and may also be observed in the beard, eyebrows, or any other part of the body.

The size of such spots in the commencement of the disease is about that of a shilling, but sometimes much larger; and when there exists a large number of spots, they often form most curious figures.

The disease is more common in females than in males, and no age is exempted from it. We find usually alterations of the general health in the same individual, who is either badly nourished, of weak constitution, or of a nervous temperament. In eighty cases observed by Mr. Wilson, fifty-seven were dependent on nutritive debility, eleven on nervous debility, nine on assimilative debility, whilst three owed their origin to local debility. The remote predisposing causes in these cases, arranged in their order of frequency, were as follows :— Scarlatina, rubeola, whooping-cough, organic disease, anxiety, fatigue and affection, pregnancy and parturition, rapid growth, anæmia, neuralgia and nervous shocks, deficient food, climate and season, congenital weakness, deranged menstruation, fever, and eczematous diathesis. The local injuries that had resulted in area were—Accidental evulsion of the hair, stinging by bees, and a bruised wound.

The cause of the affection under discussion being in the majority of cases some derangement of general health, we cannot be surprised to find the persons afflicted with this kind of baldness generally of a rather weak constitution.

The third form, depriving the whole scalp of its hair, must be distinguished from the baldness of old people; occurring in young persons, it has been named "juvenile alopecia." The mode of action is the same in both the juvenile and senile alopecia. In old age the action of the nerves, as well as the circulation of blood, becomes diminished, and as a natural consequence, the energy of transformation of substance and tissue decreases, and therefore on the one hand hair is not formed at all, and on the other, the existing hair is not sufficiently nourished and falls off. In concurrence herewith we find a head fully grown with hair in such old people only as are vigorous and strong beyond the average, and enjoy excellent health.

The juvenile baldness consists of a total absence of hair in young people, extending sometimes not only over the whole head, but affecting even the eyebrows and face. In twelve cases of this affection observed by Wilson, five affected the head alone, four the eyebrows, the eyelids, and the face, together with the head, and three the entire body. The ages of these patients ranged from five years to forty-one; five being under twenty, two between twenty and twenty-five, four between thirty and thirty-five, and the remaining case forty-one. The causes are the same as those of area, and the connexion of the two varieties is manifest by the fact that the general baldness often begins as area, forming a small spot, and extending afterwards over the whole scalp.

The disease may be congenital; this is a very rare occurrence, and then if it occurs it is generally partial.

In respect to the treatment of alopecia, it must be remembered that the falling off of the hair is not the disease, but the consequence of the same. Medical advice is therefore necessary, in order to investigate the nature of the individual case, and to find out the cause of the affliction. Hence it is evident that no general remedy is possible, and that no cure of baldness can be successful until the cause has been discovered and removed. If the patient be of weak constitution or ill-nourished, he must be strengthened; if some important functions, as digestion, &c., have been deranged, they must be restored to their normal action; if undue nervous activity be the cause, special attention must be directed to the nervous system, and it requires sometimes the most attentive consideration of the case, and a very rational treatment, in order to arrive at the desired end. Some time ago I had a lad, twelve years of age, under my care in the Farringdon Dispensary, who, in the course of a few weeks had lost his hair in such a manner as to leave the scalp entirely bald. The boy was very ill-fed, his complexion pale, and his constitution weakened. After I had procured better food and administered appropriate internal remedies, the hair soon began to grow, and the head regained its normal appearance, without my having applied any local remedy in the shape of lotion, ointment, plaster, &c.

But there are cases in which such local applications may be used with benefit, when the hair is first noticed shedding, or its growth promoted when the primary cause has been removed and formation of hair is beginning.

The relation existing between the fungi present in some cases, and the alopecia, has not been yet clearly made out, viz., whether these fungi are the cause or the effect of the disease.

There are many other diseases of the skin affecting the hair and causing it to fall out or break off, involving questions of a purely medical character, and for which proper advice must be sought. For the purpose of this book it is sufficient to show, that diseases of the hair—be they of a general or local character— do not follow any other laws than other diseases do, and that a knowledge of the whole human body in its physiological and pathological state is required in order to treat such affections successfully. This is a proposition which is self-suggestive, and which ought to be understood as a matter of course, but I state it expressly, knowing popular opinion to be in this respect very often as curious as erroneous; hence the open field for the trickery of charlatanism and deception of all kinds in the department of so-called "cosmetics." If a general knowledge were prevalent of the physiology of the hair and skin, advertisements of specifics for "making the hair grow," &c., would soon disappear from the columns of the journals.

CHAPTER XIII.

MANAGEMENT OF THE HAIR—HAIR DYES.

After what I have hitherto stated, it need not be repeated that all panaceas and appliances for the hair and skin, the composition of which is held as a secret, have no other purpose than to tax the stupidity and the ignorance of the buyer. The secret is necessary for the charlatan, lest his mixture should soon be recognised—as it generally is—as consisting of the most simple drugs, which one can get at every chemist's shop at a very much lower price than that charged by the keeper of the so-called secret. The only secret to me is, how it is possible that people should be deceived by charlatans daily, and nevertheless believe them, taking notice of their advertisements and buying their concoctions.

Let it be remembered that hair, when once altered in texture, can by no means be brought back to its normal state; that skin under no circumstances can produce hair if deprived of the hair-sacs and papillæ; that if the latter be present and the development of hair nevertheless impaired, it requires not only care but knowledge to discover the cause of that impairment, and that the treatment must tend to influence either the constitution generally or the condition of the skin; and finally, that the hair already existing is entirely out of question with respect to any treatment.

Concerning the management of healthy hair, the most simple means will prove the most beneficial. Cleanliness of the scalp, cutting the hair now and then, and keeping it moderately greased by some simple pure oil or pomatum, will suffice under all circumstances. Falling out of the hair or other abnormal phenomena are diseases, and must be treated as such.

It may, perhaps, be convenient to add some prescriptions for the preparation of oils or pomatums generally in use, and (like pomatum of Quinia, or of Tannin and Quinia) considered to act beneficially on the skin and roots of the hair.

The best means of cleansing the scalp is a weak solution of alcohol in water, or a solution of subcarbonate of soda, distilled water, and essence of vanilla.

The preparations called "Bandoline," "Fixature," &c., much used for the purpose of rendering the hair glossy and fixing the bandeaux in the required position, according to the same author, are prepared of

Gum tragacanth.
Distilled water.

To be allowed to digest for five or six hours, then strain through muslin, press, and add

Alcohol,
Rose water.

Mucilage of Cydonia and eau de Cologne are also frequently employed for a similar purpose.

Prescriptions for Oil :—

Take—Provence oil, 3 oz.
Essential oil of sweet almonds, } 2 drops
Oil of roses.   } of each.
Orange oil, 5 drops.
Lemon oil, 10 drops.

If preferred coloured, this may easily be done by digesting a little alkanet-root in it for a few days.

Marrow Oil.*

Take of—Clarified beef-marrow, 1½ oz.
Oil of almonds ¼ pt.

Melt them together and scent the mixture at will by a few drops of any essential oil—viz., bergamot, cloves, lavender, lemon, neroli, nutmeg, &c.

*Macassar Oil.**

Take of—Oil of almonds (reddened) 1 pt.

Oil of rosemary, } of each 1 drachm.
Oil of origanum, }

Oil of nutmeg, } of each 15 drops.
Otto of roses, }

Neroli, 6 drops.

Essence of musk, 3 or 4 drops.

Mix, and add alcohol drop by drop, with agitation, as long as it will bear it, or until about two fluid ounces have been added.

*Huile Comagene.**

Take of—Marrow oil, 4 oz.

Spirit of rosemary, 1½ fluid oz.

Oil of nutmeg, 12 drops.—Mix by agitation.

Prescriptions for Pomatum :—

The simplest form of pomatum consists of about two parts of hog's lard and one part of beef-suet, melted by a moderate temperature and scented with some essential oil; without the addition of scent, the mixture is known as plain pomade.

Other formulæ are :

Take—Plain pomade, 1 lb.

Provence oil, 1 oz.—Mix and scent it.

---

* The prescriptions marked thus are taken from Arnold J. Cooley's work, " The Toilet in Ancient and Modern Times." London : Robert Hardwicke. 1868.

* Take—Plain pomade, 1 lb.
        Oil of bergamot, 1 drachm.
        Oil of lemon, ¾ drachm.
        Oil of cassia, ½ drachm.
        Oil of cloves or nutmegs, 20 drops.

Stir and mix until it begins to concentrate, and then pour it into pots or bottles.

Take—Prepared beef marrow, 3 oz.
        Jasmin oil, 1 oz.
        Cinnamon oil, } 1 scruple of each.
        Bergamot oil, }
        Essential oil of sweet almonds, 8 drops.
        Oil of roses, } 10 drops of each.
        Orange oil, }

Pomatum of Quinia.

Take—Extract of cinchona bark, 1 drachm.
        Lemon-juice, ½ drachm.
        Rose ointment, 1 ounce.
        Tincture of cantharides, ½ drachm.
        Oil of lemon peel, 10 drops.
        Oil of lavender, 5 drops.

Pomatum of Tannin and Quinia.

Take—Tannic acid, 8 grs.
        Sulphate of quinia, 6 grs.
Dissolve in a sufficient quantity of rectified spirits of wine. Add—
        Liquified cocoa oil, 5 drachms.
        Provence oil, 2 drachms.

Pomatum of cantharides has been recommended for falling off of the hair. Referring to the remarks previously made on the value of such general. recommendation, I give the following formula :

> Take—Prepared beef marrow, 2½ oz.
> Oil of jasmin, ½ oz.
> Neroli, 4 drops.
> Oil of roses, 8 drops.
> Oil of sweet almonds, 2 drops.
> Balsam of Peru, ⎰ 3 drachms of
> Tincture of cantharides, ⎱ each.

For the same purpose mixtures of cantharides have been sold, and the composition held as a secret. They are generally composed as follows :

> Take—Tincture of cantharides, 2 drachms.
> Spirit of mustard, 8 drops.
> Rectified spirit of wine, 10 drachms.
> Oil of lavender, ⎫
> Oil of sweet almonds, ⎬ 5 drops of each has
> Oil of roses, ⎪ generally been re-
> Neroli, ⎭ commended. '

One teaspoonful of the mixture to be rubbed into the scalp every other day.

Hair-dyes are by no means a new invention, but have been used by the Greeks and Romans, and we are still in possession of prescriptions given for the preparation of such dyes by physicians like Galen, Avicenna, Rhazes and others.

Although a fashion has recently been revived

which was much practised by the ladies of Rome—namely, to give a light colour to dark hair—yet it is the black hair-dye which assumes the greatest importance, because in general use, and therefore the subject of speculation on the purse of the credulous, and sometimes dangerous on account of the ingredients of the mixtures used.

The requirements of a good hair-dye are— 1. That it must not be injurious to the general health. 2. That it must dye the hair, but not the skin. 3. That it must have no ill effect on the structure of the hair. 4. That it must not require a long time for the production of its effect.

A dye which possesses these four qualities has not yet been invented, for of the two principal chemicals used for staining the hair— viz., nitrate of silver and lead, the former colours the skin as well as the hair, while the latter is poisonous, and liable to cause most painful colics, and even contractions of the limbs.

Mr. Erasmus Wilson has recently commented on the subject, and we give an extract of his views as reproduced in the *British Medical Journal*, (1868, No. 412.)

" The attention which we called some time since to the new and perfect black hair dye which Dr. M'Call Anderson lately incidentally hit upon, produced a long series of commentaries from accomplished dermatologists and others well qualified to speak on the not uninteresting subject. Mr. Erasmus Wilson, a leader amongst the professors of dermatology, now enters upon and discusses the whole question in a series of very interesting observations in the *Journal of Cutaneous Medicine.* He observes, that the hair owes its property of dyeing to its porosity; which is evidently greater than its physiological structure would lead us to infer. Another of its properties— namely, the presence of sulphur in its constitution, renders it prone to darken under the use of certain mineral substances—for example, lead and mercury, whose compounds with sulphur are black. Thus, if a weak solution of lead or mercury be brushed into the hair, a certain quantity of the solution will penetrate the hair, and a dark colour will be produced in consequence of the formation of a sulphuret of lead or sulphuret of mercury. The depth of the shade of colour will depend upon the quantity of sulphur present in the hair, and as red hair and light-coloured hair contain more sulphur than dark hair, the result will in that case be comparatively greater. But where the amount of sulphur is too minute to produce the dye, science suggests the means of introducing more sulphur, as is illustrated, by a reversal of the process, in the following quotation from a paper by Dr. M'Call Anderson on eczema marginatum :—' During the treatment I accidentally discovered what promises to be the most perfect black dye for the hair which has been seen. After having used the bichloride lotion for some weeks, I changed it for the lotion of hyposulphite of soda; and the morning after the first application the hair of the part which before was bright red, had become nearly black. One or two more applications rendered it jet-black, while neither the skin nor the clothing was stained. I saw this patient a couple of weeks later, and there was not the least deterioration of colour; although, of course, as the hair grows the new portions will possess the normal tint.' The reason of the escape of the epidermis, while the hair was so thoroughly dyed, is, that it contains no sulphur. Mr. Balmanno Squire, in a commentary on the above process, observes that if instead of the hyposulphite of soda one of the more common mordants be employed— say, for example, the sulphide of ammonium— 'instead of a black, a bright red colour will result. The *modus operandi* of Dr. Anderson's dye is this. The hyposulphurous acid, on being liberated from the soda, decomposes into sulphurous acid and sulphur. The sulphurous acid reduces the bichloride of mercury to the chloride, and the sulphur converts the chloride into (black) sulphide. The effect of sulphide of ammonium on bichloride of mercury is to produce the (red) bisulphite which is the common vermilion of commerce.' Another commentator on 'hair-dyes' observes that, with the barbers, the 'sheet-anchor appears to be lead and lime.' And again, it is recommended to 'first wash the hair with a solution (ten grains to the ounce) of nitrate of silver; then use a weak solution of pyrogallic acid, and wash.' An interesting article on the subject, from the pen of an able chemical writer, Dr. Scoffern, may be found in the May number of *Belgravia,* under the head of Cosmetics for the Hair. Dr. Scoffern reminds

us that the Persians employ indigo to procure
a blue-black dye, and the Turks and Egyptians
a 'pasty writing-ink,' composed of pyrogallic
acid in combination with a native ore of iron,
while in the West the chief constituents of
hair-dyes are metallic bodies and walnut-juice.
The metals chiefly in use as 'capillary chro-
matics' are silver, lead, and arsenic; while
others applicable to a similar purpose are
gold, bismuth, iron, copper, cadmium, titanium, uranium, and molybdenum. Lead, in
its crudest form, is represented by the leaden
comb; but as the progress by this means is
slow, a compound of oxide of lead or litharge
with lime, and made into a paste with water,
is more commonly employed. This is smeared
on the hair at night, the evolved gases being
imprisoned by an oil-silk cap, and in the
morning the dried paste is brushed out, and
the hair refreshed with pomatum. Or, if a
so-called brown, a 'smothered' or 'fusty
black' be required, the paste should be mixed
with milk instead of water. The night is
preferable for these remedies, because the hair
is supposed to exhale more sulphur at this
period than during the day. These preparations remind us of a lotion in common use at

the present time, consisting of a drachm of acetate of lead with twice the quantity of sulphur to half a pint of water. The nitrate of silver is another common form of dye, but is open to the objection of staining the skin, and, in fact, everything it touches, and also of becoming iridescent on exposure to light, producing, as Dr. Scoffern observes, a 'chromatic play of tints' which is very undesirable. Bismuth presents the same characteristics as lead, but is not much used; and when iron is employed to produce a black tint, it requires for its mordants either the pyrogallic acid or the hydrosulphate of ammonia. Brown is produced by the chloride of gold alone, as also by a solution of sulphate of copper with a mordant of the prussiate of potash (ferrocyanide of potassium); and titanium, uranium, and molybdenum, judged by their chemical behaviour, would give rise to similar results. The 'golden yellow colour,' so much in fashion of late, is produced by a solution of arsenic with a mordant of the hydrosulphate of ammonia. And cadmium would probably give rise to a similar result. In the case of dyeing the lighter tints, however, it becomes necessary to submit the hair to a process of bleaching, which is commonly effected by a solution of one or other of the alkalies, by chlorine, by the chloride of soda or lime, or by sulphurous acid, bisulphate of magnesia or lime, or peroxide of hydrogen. In general, the dyes requiring mordants do not stain the epidermis."

Hair-dyes are sold in the shops which profess to restore the original colour of the hair— some of them are known as hair-restorers, and sold at a high price, but the materials of which they consist may be bought for a few pence.

The following Formula approaches as near as possible the composition known under the name of

ROSSITOR'S HAIR RESTORER.

Take—Acetate of lead, 45 grains.
　　　Precipitated sulphur, 2 drachms.
　　　Glycerine, 6 drachms.
　　　Rose-water, 10 ounces.

Mix the sulphur intimately with the glycerine until it is equally distributed, then add the rose-water in which the lead has been dissolved.

A careful examination of the facts laid down in this work, will show that all dyes have only a mechanical effect on the hair already formed, but no effect on that which is in formation.

THE END.